For Danny and John

1

THE MASTER PLAN

I watched as Finn Fitzpatrick placed a wad of fifty-euro notes in a neat pile on the locker-room floor. He huddled closer. Then, with a flick of his golden hair, he casually announced that he was setting up a bank.

Nobody blinked.

'Huh. Cop on, Finner,' said Gabriel O'Rourke finally. You could always rely on Gabe to break any silence. The mouthy sod.

But Finn's face didn't crack. He was serious. He usually was when it came to money.

'Where'd you get that cash?' I said, immediately suspicious.

'Savings, Luke boy.'

I stared at the pile of glimmering paper, momentarily transfixed by the smell of crisp new notes.

'This is cra-zy,' said Pablo Silva, a recent recruit to our gang. 'He's joking, right?'

Nobody replied. Not even Gabe.

'Hey, Finn, give the money to me, you crazy cowboy,' Pablo continued, swiping at the cash, his dark eyes flashing with amusement. 'I've no problem spending it.'

Finn placed his index finger firmly on the pile of notes. 'Ah, that's just it, boys. I won't be giving the money away. I'll be loaning it, right, Koby?'

Over in the corner, Koby Kowalski nodded.

So Koby knew about this plan. What a shock. Finn had nerves of steel, but the brains for this stuff – not so much.

'Lending money for a profit,' Koby said.

'Exactly,' said Finn, beaming and rubbing his hands. 'Just like a proper bank.'

It turned out that this light-bulb moment had come to Finn in the dentist's chair of all places. Probably from all the drugs they had to pump into him when they yanked his tooth out.

Finn threw out the facts as he saw them. 'So I'm sitting there, tooth half out, blood everywhere, in serious feckin' agony –'

I yawned loudly. Blood everywhere. Typical Finn. Bet he was put to sleep for it. I glanced at the time, wondering how long this story was likely to go on for. Finn sounded like he was gearing up for an epic.

'When Boy Wonder popped into my head,' he went on.

'Jeez, sounds like you were hallucinating big time, Finner,' said Gabe with a roar.

'Shut it, Gabe,' said Finn, jabbing him.

'Who?' mumbled Pablo to me, lost.

'Boy Wonder, the boy band,' I said. 'From the TV show.'

'So, there's Boy Wonder, racing around in my brain. And then – BOOM – Mona Lisa Murphy's there too.' Finn's face lit up. He stopped talking, as if no further explanation was required.

Nobody reacted, except for Koby, who was nodding enthusiastically. Clearly, he'd heard this story before.

Finn frowned. 'C'mon lads, d'you not see it?'

Suddenly I remembered: the back of maths class. Annalisa

Murphy going on and on and on about the Boy Wonder concert, how she'd do anything to go but she didn't have the funds to cover the ticket. Her parents had refused to give her an advance on her pocket money because she'd been caught mitching school.

'Two words: C-A-S-H F-L-O-W,' Finn spelt out dramatically.

'Cash flow,' Koby clarified, probably for Gabe.

'That's Mona Lisa Murphy's problem,' said Finn knowingly.

'One of her problems,' I said to Pablo.

Finn was on a roll. 'A problem we can solve.'

Gabe grunted, shaking his head and fiddling furiously with his phone. He didn't get it. Not the brightest light around, our Gabe.

The bell rang.

I sighed. Next class: Spanish. And I'd no homework done again. Me and Mrs Walsh were on a collision course. Unless I got my act together, she was going to sting me, and soon. I liked Spanish. I just didn't like Mrs Walsh much. And the feeling seemed to be mutual.

'What d'you think, Luke?'

I looked up. Finn was staring at me.

'So you're gonna be a loan shark,' I said with a grin, jumping up and stretching.

The others laughed. Truth was I'd heard it all before. It was just another of Finn's madcap ideas.

'Tosser.' Finn rolled back and flung his beanie hat in my face. But he was smiling. He obviously figured I'd come on board, eventually.

Suddenly I smelt lemons. Emily Clarke appeared beside me.

'What are you guys up to?' she said, eying us suspiciously, her gaze resting momentarily on Pablo. She treated him to one of her dazzling smiles.

Her eyes widened. She'd spotted the money. 'Holy cowbells. What's going on?'

I grabbed my bag and left them to it. The bell was long gone. The last thing I needed was another late detention. It'd make Mrs Walsh's day.

2
SPEEDY O'NEILL

It was lunchtime and we were messing around on the basketball court. As Pablo, Gabe and I kicked a football to each other, Koby and Finn discussed the pros and cons of the bank lending money to Speedy O'Neill.

'Speedy's run up quite a tab in the school canteen,' said Finn.

No surprise there. Speedy had a habit of reckless spending, mostly to fill his stomach. He could eat for Ireland, but still run a length of the pitch faster than anyone. And he was a skinny little fecker.

'Yeah,' said Koby. 'Big Peggy put a stop to that when she saw how much he owed. Now he has to pay it all back.'

I was curious. 'How much does he owe?'

'Sixty quid,' said Koby.

I whistled.

'Most of the canteen's profits come from Speedy, though,' Koby added.

'The guy's a horse. He probably eats more in a day then I'd put away in a week,' I said.

'Apparently Big Peg gave Speedy an ultimatum,' Koby went on. 'He has to pay it back or she calls in his parents.'

'Yeah, Speedy's goin' mad. His parents are really weird about other people knowing their business, his ma being a councillor and all. Afraid it'll get into the newspapers.'

Everyone stared at Gabe, provider of this golden nugget.

Finn snorted. 'The newspapers, ser-i-ous-ly. Who do they think they are? The Beckhams?'

I made a run for the ball. 'Speedy has a right foot like Becks. Straight into the top corner, wha'.'

'That's a Neymar special, Lukey boy,' Finn said, watching the ball veer nicely towards Gabe's head.

'Speedy's dad owns a few businesses too, remember,' said Koby knowingly. 'So they've got funds.'

That swung it. Speedy was in.

'What'll we charge, though?' Finn pondered aloud. 'That's the question.'

'Feck sake, Gabe.' I watched as the soccer ball flew over the fence.

'Gabe, you crazy fool. What kind of a shot was that?' said Pablo, already running towards the gate to retrieve the ball. 'Crazy. Crazy.'

'It'd probably help if you took this off,' I said, tapping on Gabe's trademark black motorbike helmet.

'Take it off? Fat chance. Gabe probably wears that yoke to bed at night,' said Finn.

Gabe shrugged his shoulders and took out his phone.

'Ten per cent,' said Koby eventually, having given Finn's question considerable thought. 'We'll charge ten per cent. So you'll make one euro on every tenner you lend out.'

Gabe piped up. 'One euro. Jeez, you won't get rich quick, lads.'

Finn kicked the gravel. 'Gabe, stick to *Angry Birds*, you donkey.'

Gabe chortled.

Finn glared at Koby.

'Look, we need to keep the terms low and short at first,' said Koby. 'We'll trial run with Speedy.'

'Thirty squids is all Speedy's getting to start with,' said Finn, nodding decisively.

I looked up. 'How much did he want?'

'The full sixty. First rule of banking: never lend the full amount.'

'What are the other rules?' I said, suddenly amused. Finn's proclamations needed to come with a health warning.

Finn laughed. 'Not a bloody clue.'

'I thought you were doin' honours business studies,' I said, 'with Raffo.'

Koby grinned. 'The genius.'

'Unconfirmed genius,' said Finn, rolling his eyes.

I opened my mouth to reply.

'I know, I know,' Finn continued, 'Mr Rafferty's a member of MENSA, chart toppin' IQ, and he's published three bestselling books, and he's a micro-celebrity now, spreading his love of economics across the airwaves. But as I always say –'

'What would a member of MENSA be doing teaching algebra and balancing spreadsheets to a bunch of farmers in the middle of nowhere?' I finished for him.

Finn nodded. 'Exactly.'

'Heads,' yelled Pablo, kicking the ball back over the fence.

We spent the next while taking shots at an imaginary goal, with Gabe acting as goalkeeper – or, more accurately, a target standing vaguely in the area of the goal while playing games on his phone.

'So, you in, Luke?' said Finn, walking towards me at the end of the kick-about.

I didn't reply. I still wasn't convinced. Odds were this idea would end up buried in the graveyard alongside our other grand schemes that had failed miserably over the years. And because this involved cold, hard cash, there were going to be casualties. Admittedly, a little part of me also relished taking the risk, just like Finn. And that was precisely what he was counting on.

I squinted and raised my hand to block the glare of the sun, finally meeting Finn's persuasive stare.

'Come on, Luke. Even Koby's in.'

I raised my eyebrows. 'I'm sure he didn't need much encouragement. Koby gets emotional at the sight of a calculator.'

Finn grinned. 'That's why I need you on board, Lukey. Look what I'm surrounded by. I need you to save my feckin' sanity.'

I followed his nod over to where Koby was enthusiastically explaining the physics behind the perfect keepy-uppy to a somewhat perplexed Pablo.

Finn stepped closer. 'You don't want to miss out on this opportunity, Luke. It's pure gold. I can feel it.'

I'd heard those lines before.

'Plus you might need the money,' he added, in a low, conspiratorial voice.

I turned back to him. 'What d'you mean?'

Finn shrugged innocently. 'Nothing.'

I could usually tell when Finn was playing me. I watched as he carefully reshaped the top of his blond hair into his famed Mohican cut.

The reality was my involvement would give this idea some credibility. Finn had unapologetically trampled over a few too many people in the past. His reputation wasn't exactly flawless. Finn knew it and I knew it. And that was my bargaining tool.

We walked towards the gate.

'All right,' I said. 'How much will I need?'

'One-fifty,' replied Finn immediately.

I had €463.76 in savings. Not a huge dent.

'Not a chance,' I said. 'Seventy-five.'

'One hundred.'

'OK.' I was happy. I knew Koby and Finn had both paid in one-fifty.

I stopped. 'Profits split three ways?'

Finn made a face. 'Well, thirty per cent, thirty per cent – and forty per cent for me. After all, it was my idea.'

Muppet.

3

THE CONTRACT

Finn and I were sitting in the changing rooms, watching Speedy O'Neill wolf his way through an entire box of cereal bars. A pre-training snack. There were already three wrappers on the floor.

'Speedy, here's the deal,' said Finn. 'We lend you thirty euro. And you pay us back over three weeks, eleven euro a week.'

Speedy nodded, his mouth full.

Finn produced a piece of paper and thrust it towards him. 'Sign here.'

I intercepted the sheet, eyeballing Finn.

'What the hell is this?' I hissed.

I didn't appreciate being left out of stuff, especially as I'd volunteered my savings to start this venture. All right, I hadn't physically handed over any cash yet. I was happy to let Finn and Koby use up their stash first. Plus this test run with Speedy could be a total disaster. But if we were in this, we were in this together. No splinter groups.

I scanned the page:

26 September
Loan – €30.00 @ 10% interest

I, Speedy O'Neill, commit to pay FFP Bank €33.00 over the next 3 weeks (€11.00 each week).

Signature:

This had Koby written all over it. Finn could barely power on a computer.

Finn could see I was fizzing. We moved over slightly, out of earshot of the preoccupied Speedy.

'Sorry, Luke. Me and Koby did this up real quick last night on his laptop. We thought Speedy had to sign something, like a contract. Otherwise we might never get any money back from the mad fecker.'

I sighed. 'All right. But we need to sort this.'

'Relax, I'll organise a meeting soon,' said Finn, taking back the sheet.

I caught Finn's arm. 'Hold on. FFP Bank?'

'Finn-Fitz-Patrick: FFP. It's genius.'

I rolled my eyes. I hoped he was joking, but there wasn't a hint of sarcasm.

'What if I don't pay it back?' Speedy piped up from behind.

Finn and I stared at each other, momentarily stumped. Good

point. Speedy wasn't as lightweight as he looked. I glared at Finn. I was happy to leave him to deal with this. After all, he and Koby had totally sidestepped me on this contract business.

Finn turned to Speedy, who was busy removing pieces of cereal bar lodged in his back teeth as he paced up and down the room. He always looked wired, like he had just downed two cases of energy drinks.

'Speedy, don't play with us. We know that Big Peg is this close to knocking on your front door. You need this cash.'

Speedy burped loudly. 'Hey, relax, Finn boy, I'm just asking.'

Finn fumbled in his pockets, found a pen and started scribbling.

'Here,' he said finally, handing me the updated contract.

26 September
Loan – €30.00 @ 10% interest

I, Speedy O'Neill, commit to pay FFP Bank €33.00 over the next 3 weeks (€11.00 each week).

Signature:

€3 added for every week you're late.
So pay up, ya monkey!

Speedy had signed the contract and eaten all six cereal bars by the time the rest of the lads arrived for training.

4

THE AGM

Bang.

Bang.

Bang.

I tipped the football against my bedroom wall, a little harder this time. Couple more minutes should do it.

Bang.

Bang.

The kitchen door opened.

'*Luuuuuke!* Stop with that football in the house,' Mam yelled. The sound of a door slam reverberated up the stairs.

Tip.

Tip.

Tip.

'Luke. Seriously. STOP. IT. NOW.'

Time to go.

I thundered down the stairs two at a time and poked my head around the kitchen door. Mam and Dad were at the table, heads bent over the laptop, whispering. Every evening it was the same lately. Something was definitely up.

'OK if I head out for a while?'

Only Mam looked up, still irritated. 'Where?'

'Finn's house. Just to get some homework,' I said vaguely.

'Yes, go. Give us some peace.'

Bingo.

I bolted before she changed her mind.

$ $ $

'Hey, girlfriends.' Emily appeared at the school gate, with Pablo in tow.

'What's she doing here?' Finn barked.

Pablo jumped in quickly. 'Hey, c'mon, man. She can help.'

Emily mouthed a 'Thank you' to him in deliberate slow motion.

'Finn, don't be a total clown. You know I'm top at pretty much every class in our year,' she said matter-of-factly.

Finn looked at me.

'The girl's a genius,' I said, laughing.

'I think "child prodigy" is the phrase you're looking for, Luke,' she said, grabbing her hair and twisting it into a knot on top of her head, grinning.

Truth was, I welcomed Emily's involvement. Yes, she was intelligent – almost as intelligent as Koby – but with the street smarts to match. And more importantly, being Finn's cousin, she had an ability to keep him in check that the rest of us simply didn't. Plus, the girl had a red belt in judo. Enough said.

'Well?' she said, turning and glaring at Finn.

'This is a serious business, Em – a council of war, not speed-dating for dummies, know what I mean?' Finn nodded towards Pablo.

Emily scanned the group and pulled out her phone. 'Hmm, no Cats McMahon, Finn. I'll just text her and tell her about this meeting. She'll be extremely upset that she didn't get an invite.'

Finn's eye's narrowed. 'Em, don't you dare –'

'Oh, yes, of course. Caterina probably wouldn't approve of all this, would she? Her being a proper little lady of the manor. Maybe she'll finally kick you to the kerb for good. Or that grand horse of hers might,' said Emily, hands on hips.

I smirked. Emily really knew how to push Finn's buttons.

She plumped up her lips, ready to mimic Caterina's accent. 'Remind me, Finny, is it on or off with you two these days?'

'Em!' Finn snapped.

Gabe pulled up the visor on his helmet. 'It's on. Finn bought her a hot chicken roll yesterday.'

Emily sniggered. 'Get you, big spender.'

I whistled. 'Hot chicken roll, eh. Splashin' the cash.'

Finn reached out and slammed Gabe's visor back down.

Emily dangled her phone in Finn's face. 'So?'

Finn gritted his teeth, exasperated. 'Right, you can stay, Em.'

Emily had her eyes on the prize. 'What's in it for me, Finners? To keep quiet?'

Finn sighed. 'A small percentage, like Pablo and Gabe.'

I glared at Finn. Another curve ball. How many others did he plan to cut our profits with?

'Guys, seriously, I need to be home soon,' said Koby impatiently, tapping his watch.

Finn nodded authoritatively. 'Koby's right. We need to move. C'mon.'

We followed Finn to the back of the car park and hopped the wall into the narrow lane that ran parallel to the main street.

Finn stopped at a rusty metal door. He fiddled with a key in the lock, then kicked the door in – just for show. 'Get in, quick. It's one of the shop units on Mam's books. Been empty for ages.'

'So you took the keys?'

Being an estate agent, Finn's mother regularly left big bunches of keys lying around their house.

'Borrowed, Luke. Borrowed.'

Emily pinched her nose. 'Ughhh.'

'Shhh,' Finn hissed, shoving her through the door.

Once we were all inside, he pulled out a torch.

'Nice,' I muttered, surveying the surroundings. All four walls were covered in white tiles right up to the ceiling. We were surrounded by stainless steel – counters, tables and shelves – all covered in a layer of green dust that looked suspiciously like mould. Worryingly, my feet were sticking slightly to the floor.

'Yeah, it used to be a butcher's,' said Finn, shining a light on the cobwebbed ceiling.

Emily shuddered. 'That explains the smell.'

'Find something to sit on,' Finn said, grabbing the only stool in the room.

'Lads, fancy a burger?' Gabe appeared, wearing a filthy black-and-white-striped apron and white plastic gloves. He lunged at Emily for a bear hug.

She squealed. 'Get off. That stuff could be contaminated.'

'Feck sake, Gabe. Quit it or you're out,' said Finn, ripping off the apron. 'And take off that damn helmet.'

Gabe slumped onto the table.

'Now, let's get this party started.' Finn stood up and cleared his throat, like he was the president of the United States about to give a keynote speech. I swallowed a laugh. Looking away,

I locked eyes with Emily and we exchanged the same silent message. What a prat.

'Err … I've gathered you all here today for the first official meeting of FFP Bank –'

Someone sniggered.

'The official opening of FFP Bank,' Finn continued, ignoring it. 'So the first thing is: nothing goes beyond these walls. Between the six people here, I mean.'

He regarded us sternly. Emily, Koby and I nodded.

'Gabe, are you listening? Put that poxy phone down.'

'Yeah, that's cool, Finn boy,' Gabe replied, both eyes still fixated on his phone. He was a flippin' addict.

I wasn't sure why Gabe was here. He was a liability. But Finn had assured me that somebody of Gabe's physique and aggressive tendencies might come in handy at some stage. I hoped not.

'Pablo?' said Finn, turning to him.

'Sure, sure, Finn,' said Pablo. 'I can keep my mouth shut.'

This final comment seemed to throw Emily into a spasm.

I didn't question why Pablo was here. OK, Pablo couldn't raise the cash, but he would bring in the girls. For that reason alone, Pablo had been welcomed into the gang with open arms.

When I tuned back in, Finn was still blabbering on about everyone keeping their mouths shut. I needed him to get to the point.

'So, what's the story with Speedy?' I interrupted.

'He's paid up, right, Koby?' said Finn.

Koby nodded. 'Eleven euro this week and last. One week to go.'

Not too shabby. 'Where's Speedy getting the money? Is he on a diet?'

'He's got a job washing cars at his cousin's garage,' Emily said.

I looked up, surprised. This was news to me. I couldn't imagine Speedy holding down any type of steady work. I'd always presumed his constant food supply was courtesy of Ma and Pa Speedy.

'Yeah, that's why we gave him the loan. Steady income,' said Koby soberly. 'He is what we call a solid investment.'

'You been swallowing English dictionaries again?' I said to Koby.

'Wikipedia is my friend.' He grinned at me. 'So, just remember: solid investments only. Nothing risky. We don't hand over cash to anyone who can't pay us back.'

Koby fished into his bag and pulled out a block of Post-it notes and a pen. He scribbled on a Post-it and stuck it on the wall: ROCK SOLID.

'Rock solid, like … Amy Cahill,' Finn said, winking.

Amy Cahill was the captain of the girl's junior rugby team. A tank.

I nodded. 'Yeah, I pity the poor sod who has to face her down on the pitch.'

'Rock solid, like you and Cats, eh?' Emily threw at Finn, twisting her two fingers in a knot.

'Funny.' Finn tossed the filthy apron over her head.

Finn pointed at me. 'Rock solid, like Luke's dance moves.'

Everybody burst out laughing. Even Gabe was suddenly engaged with the conversation. Finn hopped up and started throwing out some exaggerated android moves. Gabe joined in, flinging his arms about wildly.

'C'mon, I'm not that bad,' I said.

'Lukey, you burn up the floor.'

'Aw, he just needs to find his swagger,' Emily said, sticking up for me.

Koby tapped impatiently on his pad. 'Hello, can we keep going?'

Once things had calmed down, I asked the million-dollar question, despite already knowing the answer. It was written all over Finn's smug face. 'So, verdict? Are we going ahead with this?'

'Too bloody right we are,' said Finn quickly.

I looked to Koby for a more impartial answer. He hesitated. I narrowed my eyes. I definitely saw him hesitate. But then he nodded. 'We can make money at this, Luke. The numbers add up. But the key is to stay small. Small amounts over a few weeks, nothing too big or that drags on for too long.'

I nodded. 'Good call, Kob. Sounds sensible.'

'So we're agreed. Stay small,' Koby repeated, eyeballing Finn.

Finn flicked Gabe's earlobe. 'Like Gabe's brain.'

'Like Finn's ego – NOT,' Emily said.

'Like Emily's feet – NOT,' Finn hit back.

We all stared at her feet. Admittedly, they were quite large for a girl.

'Ha, ha. Perfect to give you a good kick with, Fitzpatrick,' said Emily.

'And remember, short loans. Short … like … hmm … like –' Koby struggled, drawing blanks.

'Like Gabe's attention span,' Finn said, rolling his eyes.

'Or … like your famous modelling career, Finn, remember?' I added, recalling Finn's brief stint as a model in a kids' clothing catalogue when he was five.

Emily struck a pose. 'He still introduces himself as an "ex-model", don't ya, Finn? Part of the fashion in-dust-try.'

Everyone fell around laughing, except Pablo, who just looked lost.

'Or like Luke's goal tally last season,' Finn retaliated, slapping me on the back.

I stuck out my tongue. 'Funny.'

He had a point, though. I was off form last season. Barely saw the back of the net. But I'd been putting in the training all summer. Roll on our first match.

'Listen, just remember – small,' said Koby wearily.

'And short,' said Emily.

More Post-its: SMALL. SHORT.

My phone vibrated in my pocket. Three missed calls from Mam. Followed by one angry text wondering where I was.

Suddenly I was irritated. We were just time-wasting here. We had no real gameplan. 'Who the hell are we going to lend to?' I wondered aloud. 'Seriously, lads.'

'Well, Speedy needs another wad to pay off Big Peggy. He thinks he can get the rest from the car washing,' said Finn.

I persisted. 'But we can't have a bank with just one lousy customer. That's not a bank: it's just a bunch of fourteen-year-olds playing shop.'

From the floor, Gabe snorted loudly. Not sure if it was at my comment or some side-splitting moment in his game.

'We could put the word out to the football team first?' I said.

'Yeah, at least we know those lads,' said Koby.

'What d'you think, Finn?' He was unusually quiet.

'Yeah.' Finn paused. 'Should we not just let rip and tell everyone?'

Typical Finn. Always flyin' ahead. 'Cop on, Finn. We'd be the joke of the school.'

Koby shook his head. 'No, we only lend to people we know.'

Koby paused, deep in thought, and then wrote STRANGER DANGER and stuck it on the wall. Koby was a top man, quiet but sound. And smart as hell. He'd surely keep control of this thing.

'Yeah, exactly. We can't go handing out our money to any slacker,' I said, reviewing the Post-its.

'All right, lads, chill. I get it,' Finn said, scowling.

Koby glanced in my direction. 'So same terms and conditions as Speedy's loan?'

'Terms and conditions. Listen to you, Mr Financial Controller,' said Finn, still stung.

'Yeah,' I said, ignoring Finn.

'Which are?' said Emily.

'Ten per cent fee on every loan. And a three-euro penalty for every late week,' Koby replied, reaching for another Post-it.

Suddenly, Gabe scrambled to his knees and flicked two crumpled twenty euro notes in my direction. 'Catch.'

I grabbed it. 'What's this?'

'The weekly laundry money. For the hurling team kit.'

I frowned. 'Why are you givin' it to me?'

'Lads, I've an announcement to make,' Gabe said, puffing out his chest. 'I wanna start savin' me cash.'

Finn snorted. 'Ha. What cash? Let's see, how many times have I subbed you this week already? Three? Four times?'

Gabe pointed to the money absently. 'And that's my first lodgement. You'll sort me out, right?'

Finn punched Gabe's shoulder lightly. 'Mates' rates, you mean? Not on my watch.'

I held up the money. 'So, big man, how'd you plan to pay for the launderette? You can hardly rock up to the next match with a bag of smelly gear. The team won't be too impressed.'

Gabe waved his hands. 'Nah, Luke, man, I never actually bring the kit to the launderette. Nobody does. Ma washes it for me.'

Finn spun around sharply. 'Stall it. You're sayin' that the coach gives out laundry money every week.'

Gabe nodded. 'My turn this week.'

'And nobody actually brings the kit to the launderette?' said Finn.

'They all bring it home for their mammies to wash,' I finished, staring at the twenties. An uneasy feeling crept over me. I wondered if we should care where the money came from.

'Eh, hello, isn't that stealing?' said Emily, voicing my concerns.

Koby flinched. 'Reinvesting is a better word.'

'Spreading the love around, nothin' wrong with that,' said Finn, whipping the notes from my fingers. He reached over and grabbed Gabe's hand and shook it roughly. 'Meet our first savings customer, lads. Mr Gabriel O'Rourke. Welcome to FFP Bank.'

5
THE TELETUBBIES

Finn threw his sandwich on the table and grabbed a seat. 'Guess who? Slider Curley. Alan Quinn. Fudge Lonergan.'

I almost choked on my chocolate muffin. 'The Teletubbies. No way.'

Slider, Alan and Fudge were already close to legendary status in our year, nicknamed after their epic paint fight last year when they snuck into the art-supply cupboard and later emerged covered head to toe in bright red, yellow and blue paint.

'Waaay. I'm serious.'

'What the hell were they at this time?' I wondered aloud. Topping the paint-fight saga would rocket them into the stratosphere.

'Get this: they set fire to the recycling bin,' said Finn, between bites.

'Ha, brilliant. The cowboys.' Pablo laughed and banged his fist on the table, spilling everyone's drinks.

Finn grabbed his rolling can. 'Whoa, calm it, Pablo.'

'When the fire alarm went off, I was sure it was the usual drill. Our geography class didn't move for at least five minutes,' I said.

Finn nodded giddily. 'We were in maths. Raffo was less than

impressed that we were being evacuated. He was just gettin' stuck into one of his bumper editions: geometry.'

'And then the whole school was sent home. Sweet.'

Finn sat back. 'Missed double English. And I'd no essay done. Got off nicely there.'

I popped a chocolate chip in my mouth. 'The Tubbies did us all a favour.'

'They're suspended for a month,' said Finn.

'What happened exactly?' I said.

'They were sent out to the bins with all the recycling stuff and started messin' around with pieces of cardboard and a cigarette lighter,' said Finn animatedly. 'The rest is history.'

I grinned. 'The Teletubbies go green.'

Everyone laughed.

'Wait, lads, it gets better,' said Finn. 'You won't believe what they did then. Only wheeled the bin inside the sheds.'

'Really?' said Pablo, scratching his head. 'They brought the fire inside. Why?'

I shook my head. 'They're lunatics. End of.'

'Course it totally slipped their minds that the school installed those outdoor security cameras over the summer,' Finn added.

Pablo whistled. 'Ho-ho, so it's all caught on camera. Nice.'

I pulled a face. 'Seriously, though, you'd think they'd keep a low profile after all the grief they got last year.'

Finn's eyes widened. 'I know. It's only October and the Tubbies are already up the creek.'

I nodded in agreement. They'd be lucky to see out the school year at this rate.

'Lads, did you hear?' I looked up to see Koby, his cheeks

flushed with excitement, wearing an oversized bright purple raincoat.

We all murmured.

Koby flopped down next to me. 'But did you hear what Powder Keane said?'

I shivered involuntarily. I'd crossed paths with Powder Keane – named after his whiter-than-white hair – our commander-in-chief at St Patrick's Community College, on more than one occasion. He was a monster of a man, an ex-rugby player, rumoured to have once pulled a bloke's ear off with his teeth on the pitch. Probably not true, but utterly believable.

'The shed is ruined. Plus the bins. Powder's making them pay for all of it,' said Finn.

Koby was almost bursting to speak. 'Not only that. They have to cough up for the fire brigade call-out fee too.'

Finn's eyes glazed over. 'Really?' I could see he was already calculating the fallout in his head.

'You know what this means, don't you?' Koby said.

Finn nodded gleefully, rubbing his hands. 'Potential customers.'

'Hi, Luke.' I looked up. Katy Doyle was standing there, smiling at me, holding the remains of a hot chocolate.

'Oh, hi, Katy,' I managed self-consciously. All the lads were gawking at me.

'Smooth,' Finn mouthed, kicking me under the table.

'Lads.' Katy finally acknowledged the others, still looking my direction, though. 'Did ye hear about the Teletubbies and the fire? Everyone's talking about it.'

Stratosphere status.

'Anyway, gotta go. Later.'

'Hiii, Kaaatyyy. Byyyeee, Kaaatyyy,' they all chorused once she'd left.

'Shut the hell up,' I hissed, watching her pay at the till.

'I think you've an admirer there, Lukey boy,' said Finn, ruffling my hair.

'Bog off, Finn.' I didn't want to start encouraging anything.

Finn stuck out his tongue. 'Touchy.'

'What's the story with the coat, Kob?' I said, changing the subject. It was so … purple.

'Got it in Lost Property. Emergency. I'll put it back tomorrow.'

I should have guessed. Koby was always dipping into the Lost Property temporarily. I was waiting for the day when he showed up wearing something of mine.

Koby fished into the coat pocket, produced a folded piece of paper and slid it into the centre of the table.

Finn made a grab for the sheet, excited. 'Don't tell me –'

Koby nodded. 'Yeah, that's the list of sign-ups so far.'

Finn whistled. 'For once, Gabe's the superstar. Spreadin' the word about our savings offer. On the QT, of course.'

'Nearly half of the hurling lads are on board,' Koby said.

'A lot of launderette money coming our way, eh,' said Finn.

I scanned down the surprisingly long list of names. Somehow, I couldn't visualise Gabe in the role of the slick salesman. 'Is anyone keeping tabs on what Gabe's actually telling people?'

'Yeah, we gotta hop on that,' Finn said. 'Can't leave Gabe on a solo run.'

I scrunched my muffin wrapper into a ball and threw it at Finn. 'Knowing Gabe, he's overcooking it.'

'Yeah, free bacon butty with every savings account opened,' said Finn.

'In Gabe's world, probably a trip on the Starship Enterprise with every account opened.' I looked at the list again and then back at Finn. 'Did you ever think anyone would actually want to put money *into* the bank?'

Finn shook his head, chuckling. 'That's the shocker. I didn't think any of the lads would be that loose with their cash. How wrong was I!'

$ $ $

On my advice, we only approached two Teletubbies: Slider Curley and Alan Quinn. We bypassed Fudge Lonergan. He was a loose cannon. And Lonergan Senior was even worse. During last year's under-fourteen cup final, Fudge was given a second, legitimate yellow card for a blatant reckless tackle. Fudge's dad totally lost it, marched onto the pitch and head-butted the ref, knocking him out cold. The Lonergans were nutcases that we could do without.

'Jeez, lads, I didn't realise it was that bad,' Finn said, winking at me over Slider and Alan's heads.

Finn had arranged to meet them at the playground.

'It's a total disaster,' said Slider, running his hands through his greasy hair.

They were more wounded than I expected over the whole affair. In fact, they both looked wrecked. Powder Keane must have steamrolled right over their heads.

'So, are your parents gonna pay up?' Finn said carefully.

'Fat chance,' scoffed Alan, kicking the swing violently.

I hopped out of the way, startled. Alan was usually fairly relaxed.

'My dad just lost his job. He hasn't a bloody bean,' he said glumly.

I hadn't heard this news. Rough. I felt a pang of sympathy for Alan. At the same time, I could hear Koby's voice ringing in my ears: only lend to people who can pay us back.

Slider shook his head. 'Mine won't pay … says it's a matter of principle.'

I had guessed that might happen. Slider's da was the headmaster of the local primary school, no doubt far from happy at all the unwanted publicity.

'But we're after getting a leaflet run. From Slider's uncle,' Alan said.

I breathed a sigh of relief. OK, maybe solid investments after all.

Slider grumbled. 'Yeah, slave bloody labour. Uncle Pete saw us coming.'

'At least it's something. We have to start at 6 AM *every* poxy morning, though.' Alan winced, turning to us.

Whoa. No wonder they both looked shattered.

'Uncle Pete knew we were desperate and is only payin' us peanuts,' said Slider.

Alan nodded. 'Truth. We'll be years gettin' the cash back to Powder at this rate.'

Slider snorted, wiping his nose. 'Fat chance. Powder's demandin' payback in two weeks. Mission-bloody-impossible.'

Taking his cue, Finn stepped up. 'Lads, would you be interested in a small loan?'

Alan and Slider looked at Finn, suspicion written all over their faces.

'Sod off, Fitzpatrick,' Alan muttered eventually and turned to leave.

'Hang on, Alan. I'm serious,' said Finn, grabbing his arm. 'Tell them, Luke.'

'We've set up a bank,' I announced, feeling stupid. Granted, it did sound a bit out there.

Finn ushered them back. 'And we're open for business. For loans, that is.'

'Strictly confidential,' I said, jumping in.

We needed to work on our selling tactics. Slider and Alan weren't exactly jumping up and down with enthusiasm. And they were seriously up against it.

Alan was having none of it. 'A feckin' bank. You're some lad, Fitzpatrick.'

'The Weasel of Wall Street in the flesh,' said Slider, with a sly grin.

I ruffled Finn's hair, trying to lighten the mood. 'Harsh. He's more a woolly mammoth.'

Eventually we managed to persuade Slider and Alan to listen to our proposition. Initially they were wary. Presumed it was a wind-up. But then they came around. The simple fact was they were desperate: desperate to free themselves from Powder Keane's debt.

'You each owe Powder €112.65. So, let me think … We could give you both a loan of seventy euro?' said Finn. 'You'd be well over halfway there. You slap seventy into Powder's hand now, he might loosen his grip.'

'Agreed,' said Slider immediately.

Alan held his hand up. 'Wait, what's the catch? What are you charging?'

'Fifteen per cent. So you'd have to pay us back – €80.50,' said Finn, using the calculator on his phone.

'Over eight weeks,' I said, focusing on Koby and his Post-its.

Alan yawned and rubbed his eyes. 'All right, you've got a deal. These constant early starts are killing me.'

'Well, at least we'll have Powder off our backs,' said Slider.

Alan growled. 'And maybe a lie-in once a week.'

Suddenly I felt bad. I wondered if we were taking advantage of the lads' misfortune. But, hell, we were all winners here. Slider and Alan clawed a bit of sleep back. We made a profit. In a roundabout way, we were even doing Powder Keane a good turn.

'What about Fudge?' said Slider suddenly.

Finn made a face.

'Too much of a fruit 'n' nut,' guessed Alan, grinning.

I nodded. 'He's a total liability. And imagine getting on the wrong side of Fudge Senior!'

'Nutter,' shouted Finn, running backwards up the kids' slide.

I laughed. 'It takes one to know one, Finn, ya spoofer.'

It was only afterwards that I realised Finn had increased the terms of the loan to fifteen per cent. Right in front of me and I hadn't noticed. The snake.

6

THE HUNGER TWINS

I heard a familiar wolf-whistle.

'Luke, in here.' Koby was standing at the door of the home economics room. The smell of fresh baking alone was too good to resist. He pulled the door shut behind us.

'What's going on, Kob? I've somewhere to be in ten.'

I followed him to the back of the classroom where two bushy heads sat huddled in front of a laptop. The Sullivan sisters. Or, as Finn affectionately called them, The Hunger Twins. The tallest, skinniest girls in the world. No exaggeration, their waists were the diameter of my shins.

'Luke, you know Jo and Lucy?'

The twins glanced up and momentarily made eye contact with me. They were an odd pair: wild, curly hair, dark eyeliner, pale faces, frayed tights complete with chunky Doc Marten boots.

I half-nodded. Yes, of course I knew *of* them. Hell, the whole school knew of the Sullivan sisters. You couldn't miss them. But I couldn't recall ever talking to them much before.

'So they've developed this app,' Koby said, by way of introduction.

'We've built a software platform,' Jo cut in immediately.

'Sorry, a software platform,' said Koby, flustered. He looked a bit intimidated. Even sitting down, the twins towered over him like skyscrapers.

I gazed at the lines and lines of code on the laptop screen. I already knew that the Sullivans could write software. Last year they'd created a free map application to help newbies find their way around the school. They put a few stingers in there too. Gabe spent half a morning trying to find classroom MI5. The tool.

I stared at them all expectantly.

Eventually one of the twins, Jo, got the message and started to talk. 'We've built a software platform that compares chunks of information. Data matching.'

'Data matching,' I repeated, uncertain.

'It's a match-making app,' Koby chipped in.

'Match-making – really?' I couldn't hide the surprise in my voice. The Hunger Twins were goth girls. Not girly girls. I'd seen them around the village. Piercings. Crucifixes. Dark eyes. Not a fluffy pink Ugg boot for miles.

Jo arched an eyebrow. 'I know what you're thinking. That we're the last people you'd expect to be doing this mush, right?'

'No, no,' I lied. Totally.

'Well, it's a commercial thing. We believe this app will sell.' She stopped, waiting for my reaction.

A thought occurred to me. Did they want me to be a guinea pig in this match-making guff? Holy crap.

'Eh, great. Look, it doesn't really sound like my thing,' I muttered awkwardly. 'I'm concentrating on my football. No distractions, like girls.'

Jo smirked.

'I mean, I like girls. I'm just not into being set up or any of that stuff,' I said quickly.

The girls turned to each other and hooted with laughter.

I fired Koby a look and spun around to leave.

'Luke, hold on,' said Koby, stepping in my path. 'Jo, just tell him how it works.'

Jo nodded. 'It's a pretty simple concept: people play Cupid using this app.'

I waited.

'You can tag two people who you think will make a good match. The app will do its data-matching magic in the background, and if the app agrees with your proposed match, it will connect the two people.'

That moment, the penny dropped. The twins needed money. That's why I was here. I played with Jo's idea in my head. Actually, it wasn't half-bad.

'We asked Koby to bring you here because we've heard about your new venture,' Jo continued.

'We need a loan,' Lucy blurted, speaking for the first time.

Carefully, I turned back around to face them.

'We've done the numbers,' said Jo breathlessly, her eyes shining. She was actually quite pretty when she got excited. Well, not so scary anyway. 'It's gonna be big.'

I sat down with a bump.

'We think we can sell the app for one euro ninety-nine. Even if we got half the school to buy it, we'd make –'

'Over a grand,' I finished.

'Yeah. And I think it could be a lot bigger.'

I whistled softly. 'What's the loan for?'

'We need some capital to get the app on the market.'

'How much?'

'A hundred and fifty.'

I took a deep breath. Steep.

'I know it's a lot of money, but we really think this app –'

She was interrupted by a beeping noise.

'Damn, the cupcakes!' cried Jo, hopping up and running over to one of the ovens. 'We burnt the last batch, so we had to stay in during lunch to do them again.'

Quickly, I thought about how I was going to play this. OK, we lend the sisters the money. They'd only need to sell the app to our own year to honour the loan. Not so risky. But what if the app sold really well? What if, down the line, they added enhancements to the app and charged extra for them? Was there a way for us to capitalise on this idea? I decided to stay cool, let them do all the chasing.

'What's the app called?'

'Tagged,' shouted Jo, from the other side of the room, fiddling with a baking tray surrounded by a cloud of smoke. Clearly she did all the talking. Lucy had, by now, returned to the laptop and was tapping on the keys furiously.

'What d'you need the cash for?'

'Graphics work, mainly. We've the code done, but we need the bits on screen to look good. Professional.'

I sat back. 'So how exactly is it going to work?'

'Well, take Lucy here, for example. Imagine she wants to hook up with a guy in our year.'

'OK.' I glanced over at the frowning Lucy, totally immersed in her lines of code. Stretch of the imagination.

'And I've an idea who would be a good match for her.'

Suddenly, in a mad moment, an image of Gabe and Lucy

popped into my head. I started to smile. Gabe and Lucy, two lampoons, skipping hand in hand. Gabe, throwing shapes, trying to impress the hard-boiled Lucy. Lucy showing off her complex code to Gabe, the crazy fool. I swallowed a giggle.

Jo glared at me suspiciously. 'Do one, Luke, if you're not gonna take us seriously.'

I straightened my face. The last thing I wanted to do was rattle them. Especially as this was just getting interesting.

'So say Lucy joins Tagged. She fills in her profile – stuff like her age, description, what she likes, dislikes: sports, music, films, the usual.'

I nodded. Sounded fairly standard.

Jo waved her hand in Koby's direction. 'I look around and think, hey, Lucy and Koby here would make a great couple.'

I raised my eyebrows. Even Lucy glanced up briefly at this outlandish suggestion. Meanwhile, Koby, cheeks burning, suddenly became incredibly interested in his feet.

Jo carried on. 'I see that Koby also has a profile on Tagged. So I nominate Lucy and Koby as a match and submit. The software runs a data check, and if it agrees with this match, Lucy and Koby are tagged!'

'What happens then?'

Jo shrugged. 'Nothing.'

'What's the point of it?'

'No point.' Jo frowned at me, as if I was missing something. 'It's called fun. F-U-N. Seeing who's been tagged with who. Trust me, everyone will be talking about it. People love a bit of goss.'

Just as I suspected, the app was totally and utterly pointless. It was bound to be a mega-hit.

'We've limited membership to the school only, for now,' Jo added.

'How?'

'Simples. Got our hands on a database of every student in the school and their student ID numbers.'

I rolled my eyes. The security on the school's IT server was as loose as ever.

'Everyone has to enter their name and ID number to become a member and add a profile.'

I nodded and glanced at my watch. 'Guys, I hate to break up this party, but I've to be in class in two minutes.'

'So, what d'you think?' said Jo tentatively.

I tried to adopt a pensive look. As if I was really considering their idea.

'Not sure. It's a lot of cash to hand over. I'll probably need to speak to my associates.' That wasn't true, but I thought it made us sound more professional.

Jo swallowed a grin. 'Your associates.'

Maybe not.

There was a definite opportunity here to hop on board this bandwagon as more than just money-lenders. We'd not discussed going down the investor route. Bit of a leap, but I couldn't see Finn putting up much of a fight if our lucky numbers came up.

I decided to take the gamble. 'Thing is, if it's a success and loads of people buy the app, great. For you. But there's still a risk that nobody jumps on this. A risk that we're taking.'

I stopped. The smell of the baking was making my mouth water. Koby nodded, watching me carefully. I waved my hand discreetly. Hopefully he'd cop my change of tactics.

'Now, if there was a sweetener …' I deliberately left the sentence unfinished, waiting to see if she took the bait.

'Raspberry and white chocolate cupcake?' offered Jo, amused. She knew exactly what I was hinting at.

'You're talking about coming on board as investors? In exchange for the loan?' she said eventually, trading a cryptic sideways look with Lucy, who had momentarily peeked up from behind the screen.

I didn't reply straight away. Better to let the idea float.

Jo removed the cakes from the tin, placing them on a wire rack to cool.

'Think of us more as your financial wingmen,' I said, watching and waiting.

Jo paused. We locked eyes in silent negotiation.

'OK, what if we give you a percentage of every download?' she said, conceding. 'Ten per cent?'

Peanuts. I didn't even bother acknowledging it, just maintained direct eye contact.

She rubbed her nose self-consciously. 'Twenty per cent.'

'Thirty,' I said quickly.

'Twenty-five.'

'Deal.'

We shook on it.

'You'll need to show the app to Pablo, our IT expert. Get him to test it.'

Not surprisingly, the Sullivans had absolutely no objections. I could have sworn they almost cracked a smile at the mere mention of Pablo's name.

I grabbed a muffin and headed for the door.

'Delicious,' I mumbled back between mouthfuls.

Koby caught my arm. 'What was all that about Pablo, our so-called "IT expert"?'

I closed the door. 'Just a safeguard in case we wanna call any of the shots. The Sullivans will be like jelly around him.'

'Truth.'

'Plus when word gets out among the girls that Pablo is on the app ...'

'Yeah, it'll cause a software meltdown.' Koby grinned. 'The investment idea, though, I like, I like a lot.'

I was pleased that route got the green light from Koby, as it had come straight from left field. 'Finn'll go ape when he hears.'

Koby sniffed. 'He'll be bullin' cos he didn't think of it first.'

$ $ $

News of my deal with the Sullivan sisters soon filtered back to Finn. That evening, he ambushed me before soccer training. Of course, he was none too impressed that I had negotiated with the Sullivans on my own. Without him. A cracker of a deal. A deal that could net us some serious cash. He was fizzing but had to let on that he was genuinely pleased. It was amusing to observe.

'Feck sake, Luke. What's this I hear about me going into business with the Hunger Twins?'

'Don't you mean us, Finn? Remember our three-way split.'

'Exactly. I should've been there.'

'Cop on, Finn. You should be thanking me.'

'So, what's the deal?'

'You've not talked to Kob?'

'No, that idiot's not rung me back.'

I smiled. Koby was lying low until the dust settled. I fished my soccer boots out of my gear bag. Purposefully, I banged them together loudly, over and over, cakes of muck falling out from between the studs.

'C'mon, Luke, look, training's about to start. Spill.'

I could see this was killing Finn. He liked to be in the know about everything.

'They've created an app,' I said finally, putting him out of his misery a bit, while also being deliberately vague. 'We'll make a percentage of each sale.'

'How much?'

'Twenty-five per cent.'

'How much is the app selling for?'

'One ninety-nine.'

Finn was silent for a minute. He was doing the figures in his head.

'Not bad,' he said finally. 'But still, it's only fifty cent on every app sold. Even if they sold it to half the school –'

'That's about three hundred quid,' I said.

'Pure profit. Sounds good to me.'

'Well, not quite –'

'I'm sure I can top it, Lukey boy,' said Finn, chucking the soccer ball in my direction.

'It's not a competition, Finn, you plank.'

'Afraid you'll lose, eh?'

I kept my mouth shut. I really didn't want to go down this road with Finn. Things could spiral out of control fairly rapidly.

7

THE BUTCHER'S BLOCK

'So, let me get this straight. We are now dealing with investments, as well as loans?' Emily demanded, frowning at her sheets of paper. She'd obviously got wind of my deal with the Sullivan sisters.

'Yeah, baby,' said Finn, flexing his muscles. 'It's the money!'

'I don't remember us agreeing to that. We only discussed loans at the last meeting. Nothing about investments.'

'Back up, back up, Em. You just do the accounts. Leave the dirty work to us.'

'Danger-ous,' Emily sang at a high pitch, raising her eyebrows.

'Listen, you're getting paid, aren't you? So quit complaining,' said Finn, his eyes flashing in irritation.

Emily turned and duly thumped him hard in the arm. 'One more word, Fitzpatrick, and I'm outta here. I don't need this grief.' She crossed her arms, fuming.

Finn was about to retaliate when I caught his eye. Instead, he played the wounded card, rubbing his arm feverishly.

'Jaysus, Emily, that bloody hurt.'

'Whatever,' said Emily, looking pleased.

There was a brief pause in hostilities. I grabbed my chance. 'Emily, Kob, can one of you give us the stats?'

We were four weeks into our venture, and I really wanted to get a handle on the figures. I was worried that Finn had gone on a solo run. He looked suspiciously cheerful.

'Three loans paid up. Eight loans outstanding,' said Koby.

'Eight?' I knew it.

Finn pointed a finger at Koby. 'But we're on top of it, right?'

'Yeah. We'll be in the black once Mucker comes through.'

I pulled a face. 'Mucker McGrath. Tell me you didn't.'

Finn shrugged. 'His rugby boots got nicked. Although, I heard rumours that he left them in the changing rooms and someone chucked them, the smell was so rank. Anyway, he needed the cash to replace them without his ma finding out.'

'And before the senior cup semi-final,' Emily added.

'He's a cash cow, Lukey. It must be all that farm work during school holidays. He'll see us right after the mid-term break.'

'That's if he turns up. You might never see him again.' Mucker's school-attendance record was sporadic, to put it mildly. I'd spotted him once since we started back in September. And that was at the pitch, not even in the building.

Emily looked down through her list. 'What about Annalisa Murphy, peeps?'

My ears perked up. 'Mona Lisa. Is she lookin' for a loan?'

'Uh-huh.'

Finn waved his hands. 'Some tanning stuff she's concocted.'

'It's a home-made self-tanning oil made from coffee beans,' said Emily.'All natural ingredients. Totally organic.'

Finn looked around. 'So does she get the loan? Yes or no?'

Koby nudged Emily. 'Has she any hope of selling this tanning stuff?'

Emily scrunched up her nose. 'Eh, of course. C'mon, this is Annalisa – we all know that she's an entrepreneurial guerrilla.'

Finn snorted. 'Please. She's a mouth the size of –'

I flicked the top of a pen at Finn. 'Be fair, Mona Lisa was your inspiration for this whole bank idea.'

Finn didn't even pause. 'Go on, give her the money.'

'And then there's Rosie Byrne,' said Emily.

'The quiet one in your class with the huge glasses?' I said.

'That's the one.'

'What's she want a loan for?'

'Stationery.'

'Wha'?'

'Pencils, pens, rulers, calculators. You know – stationery.'

'It's a sideline venture,' Koby said. 'She's quite the business brain, actually.'

'Oh, does 'ickle Koby have a crush?' said Emily, rubbing his head.

Koby reddened.

'Stationery. The glamorous world of high finance, huh?' said Finn, making a face.

'Every loan counts, Finn,' said Koby, adopting a more serious tone, 'especially to the Rosie Byrnes, as they are the dependable ones.'

'Not like your playboy investments, Luke, wha'?'

I smirked at Finn. He was still bitter. 'Speaking of playboys, where's Pablo?'

'Good question,' said Finn.

Emily's face soured. 'He stayed back after school to look at the Sullivans' stupid app.'

'I don't think you've anything to worry about there, Em. The

Hunger Twins would eat Pablo for breakfast.' Finn chuckled. 'Mind you, leaving him with a dating app to play around with … now *that* I would be worried about. It's like offering candy to a baby.'

Emily looked fit to kill.

'What about these other loans?' I said quickly, before another row broke out.

Finn twitched impatiently. 'Do we really need to go through each of these one by one, Luke? Have a look at Emily's accounts. The details are all there.'

Emily handed me the sheets of paper.

I squinted. 'Any chance of getting a decent light in here, Finn?'

We were still holed up in the old butcher's shop. The smell had vanished, but it had been replaced by a thick, settled layer of dust that seemed to hover just at our heads, making visibility non-existent.

Finn ignored me, instead stretching his legs under the steel table beside him and pulling out a large block of wood with his feet.

He pushed it towards Emily. 'This is the butcher's block. Used to chop the raw flesh. I mean, meat.'

Emily immediately edged her stool away from him, shuddering. 'Keep that thing away from me, Finn. Look at all those dark stains on it. Mank.'

Finn unhooked two small clips at one side of the block, and opened it like a book, to reveal a hidden compartment, filled with rolls of bank notes.

'Our bank vault,' he announced, without a shred of sarcasm.

He placed the block in the middle of the floor. 'Tally that up, Kob.'

Koby took out the money and began counting.

'Where are you hiding this block, then?' I said anxiously. 'Seeing as you're planning on storing all our cash in it.'

Finn's face lit up. 'Ah-ha, don't you worry, Luke. Naturally, I've got that covered.'

He picked up the block and slouched over to the corner of the room. 'It just happens to fit perfectly into this gap in the floorboards. Right here.'

He let the slab down with a bang. I peeked over his shoulder.

Admittedly, from a distance, the block was concealed and looked like part of the floor. 'Not bad, Finn.'

'It's the jam. Sometimes, lads, I even surprise myself with my own feckin' brilliance.'

Finn's love-in with himself was interrupted by a shuffling noise from out the back.

'Shhh. What was that?'

A tall dark shadow appeared at the doorway, cocooned in dust.

'What the –?' Startled, I leapt back, toppling over the crate I was sitting on.

Emily and Koby screamed.

Finn backed into the wall.

'Yo-yo. This dust is awesome.'

'Gabe,' I said, breathing out heavily.

Finn leapt up. 'Gabe, for feck sake. You frightened the life out of us.'

Gabe stepped into the room. He was still dressed in full training gear, including gumshield and sports helmet.

'Or is it Darth Vader?' I grinned.

'Is he OK?' said Emily. 'He looks completely out of it'

Gabe was swaying his hands around, trying to catch dust particles.

Finn nodded. 'Yeah, he's always like this after training. It must be the intensity of the sessions. Takes him a while to come back down, to get back to normal. Well, Gabe's normal.'

Finn waved his hands in front of Gabe's face. 'Eh, hello.'

Nothing.

Finn clicked his fingers.

Nothing.

He grabbed a flattened cardboard box that was lying on the floor and swatted Gabe on the head.

Gabe blinked, finally registering Finn.

'Gabe, what are you doing here? I thought you had training.'

'Finished up early, Finn boy.'

'Take that feckin' helmet off, then.'

Gabe wedged the helmet off. A fat roll of money dropped out from behind his ear.

I made a grab for it. 'What's this?'

A sluggish Gabe kicked off his boots and slid down to the floor with a bump, wriggling his toes in his muddy socks.

Finn cracked his knuckles. 'More cash for the savings accounts, right, Gabe?'

Gabe thumped his chest in agreement.

'Gabe, you'd better be keeping track of precisely how much each person is giving you,' Emily said, following the money.

Gabe winked, tapping the side of his head. 'All up here.'

'Be afraid. Be very afraid,' Emily murmured with a smirk, catching my eye.

She had a point. We weren't exactly dealing with Albert Einstein here. Not even Einstein's distant tenth cousin. Gabe's track record with anything except existing and playing hurling was woolly. Let's face it, he even had trouble existing. It was doubtful that Gabe really had a handle on this savings business. If he did, it'd be a first.

'Gabe, what exactly are you peddling here? Spill.'

'You're wasting your time. He's gone,' Emily said to me, pointing at Gabe, who was snoring gently.

Finn flicked Gabe's cheek. 'Gabe, wake up, idiot.'

No reaction.

Finn clenched his jaw. He punched Gabe in the upper arm.

Still nothing.

Finn dived over, putting his mouth close up to Gabe's ear. 'Gabe, WAKE UP! Tell us about your savings deal.'

Gabe's eyes flickered briefly. 'Batter.'

I perked up. 'What'd he say?'

Emily shrugged. 'Butter?'

'Batter.' Gabe stirred again, lolling around in a dream-like state. 'Batter … batter … batter … batter … b … b … mmm … bat-ter.'

Emily covered her ears. 'Somebody stop him.'

Gabe shot up, eyes still closed, and, in perfect slow motion, stretched his arm out towards Emily, as if reaching for something floating past. 'Batter b-b-b-b.'

Emily whacked it away, squealing. 'Get those greasy paws away from me!'

Gabe conked out again, gradually sloping towards her.

'Ugh. Gross.' Emily pinched her nose. 'He reeks of vinegar. Like the chippy.'

'The chippy. Batter. That's it.' Finn clicked his fingers, doing a little dance. 'Smashed it.'

Gabe belched loudly.

'Animal,' Emily said, covering her nose and mouth, and diving over to the other side of the room.

'The Batter Burger Meal Deal. Gabe's favourite,' Finn said. 'Batter burger and chips for two euro.'

Emily exhaled loudly. 'I don't get it.'

Koby scratched his head. 'Me neither. What's that got to do with savings accounts?'

'Ah c'mon, lads. Batter Burger Meal for two euro. That must be the deal,' Finn translated. 'Two euro interest for every account opened?'

I made a face. 'Deal of the century.'

That'd hardly get the lads queuing up. There had to be more to it.

Koby had a go. 'Two euro for every lodgement?'

'Gabe?' Finn barked. 'You listening? Two euro for every deposit? Is that the deal?'

At this stage, Gabe was sprawled out on the floor.

Finn kicked him lightly on the shin.

Gabe's arm shot up, throwing a groggy, half-hearted thumbs-up. Then he curled up in the foetal position, a huge joker-like grin still plastered on his face.

Emily rolled her eyes. 'Seriously. His brain is a batter burger.'

$ $ $

'Dad, the Internet's down again.'

On Pablo's advice, I was trying to register for the pilot version of the Tagged app, but I couldn't connect.

Dad murmured something about checking the router later and returned to the television.

I wasn't giving in that easily. 'I've already checked the router. It's got a load of flashing orange lights. That can't be good.'

'Can I not watch the golf in peace? I'll ring the company later.'

'I need it now. It's for school,' I lied.

Dad ignored me, his eyes focused on the eighteenth hole.

'Dad?'

All of a sudden, he lost it. 'Luke, the Internet is gone, all right. No more Internet.'

'What?' I said, confused.

'We had to close the account. Money is too tight. Now will you just leave it.'

He stormed out of the room, slamming the door shut.

'Feck sake,' I muttered, wondering what the hell had just happened. Dad was the laid-back one. Mam was the fireball. I couldn't recall the last time Dad lost his temper.

I stomped back up the stairs.

Five minutes later I was sitting on the toilet logging on to Mr Kapoor's Internet connection. The Kapoors, our neighbours, were suitably ignorant on all matters of Internet security. It had taken two easy password attempts to crack it. One minor inconvenience: the Kapoor connection was only available in our upstairs toilet.

I got as far as the registration page, but then the connection crashed again. This time I gave up. My bum was killing me.

I'd have to speak to Dad when he was in better form. But lately, Dad spent his time mooching around the house like an unwanted guest. And he'd given up going in to the office. You'd swear he was under house arrest.

I knew things were bad ever since Mam's hours at the hospital had been cut to part-time. But this was getting ridiculous.

8
PADDY TARANTINO

'Paddy. Paddy. Paddy Tarantino. Paddy Tarantino. Paddy Tarantino.' Finn's voice rattled the name repeatedly as soon as I answered my phone.

I rubbed my hands over my face, attempting to dislodge the sleep from my eyes. I was knackered. My precious Saturday lie-in – the first Saturday in ages that we didn't have a soccer match – had been shattered by the sound of my mobile ringing. Over and over. Until eventually I hadn't been able to ignore it any more.

'Finn, feckin' hell, d'you know what time it is?'

'Shut up. Check your emails and ring me back.'

'Huh?'

'Just check your emails and ring me back.'

'I can't.'

'Do it.'

He hung up.

I chucked the phone across the room, reefed the duvet over my head and scrunched my eyes tight together until there were white dots. But no matter how hard I tried, I could still see the light streaming in through the slit in the curtains. I was wide awake. Bloody Finn.

Five minutes later I was sitting on the toilet logging in to my mail.

From: Fitzy
To: KobK; Luke

Paddy T
New video project
Needs capital

I clicked on the video link at the bottom of the email, hoping the Kapoors' Internet connection would hold up.

The video loaded, eventually. I pressed PLAY and waited. At first, nothing. Then, a strange clucking sound, like a hen. I wasn't all that surprised. Everyone knew Paddy Tarantino was eccentric. But he was also a top vlogger. Two years ago, Paddy posted a cat video and it catapulted him into hero status.

The story goes that a stray ginger cat used to appear on the window ledge in Paddy's bedroom and wiggle its head and bootie whenever Paddy played R&B music. The cat had an unusual shaggy mane of hair, resembling a miniature lion. Paddy had filmed the cat, manipulated the video so it appeared that the cat was singing, uploaded the footage and the rest is history. Cedric, as the cat was called, became an overnight online sensation. Since then, every one of Paddy's videos had gone viral. His video-streaming account had literally millions of hits.

Impatiently, I clicked on the video link again. A tiny chick scuttled up and down the ramp of a toy garage. Finally the chick slouched towards the camera and, in a deep, masculine voice, growled: 'Give me the money, man.'

I guessed that this was a request for funds, Paddy Tarantino style.

$ $ $

'Paddy's ready for you.'

'Great,' said Finn, leaping up.

'Great,' I repeated dryly, attempting an apologetic half-grin to the girl with the piercing green eyes and owl-like face sitting on the step below us, as Finn stumbled roughly past her.

We were sitting in Paddy's waiting room aka his basement stairs. The place was jammed. Wedged between us: two guitar-strumming hipsters and the owl-like creature. It was like some extreme talent-show audition line.

Minutes later, after following Paddy out to his yard, we stood observing six pink piglets happily guzzling in a pen.

Finn frowned. 'They're pigs.'

'No flies on you, Finn.'

'Piglets, actually,' said Paddy. 'Next big thing.'

'Pigs?' said Finn, doubtfully.

'Not pigs in general, Fitzy. These babies.'

We both turned to Paddy, hoping more information was forthcoming.

'Watch.' He fished into his pocket and pulled out a small whistle. He blew sharply and the piglets stood to order. Then he blew again and the piglets began trooping around the pen in single file, their little pink legs kicking up high.

Paddy stood back, waiting for a reaction. He blew a third time, and the lead piglet ground to a halt, with the other piglets skidding to a stop behind.

'Genius,' said Finn. I could tell by his face that he hadn't a clue.

Paddy grinned proudly. 'All my own work.'

I pointed. 'The pig at the front, he knows his stuff.'

'It's a she, actually. I call her Diana Prince.'

I thought for a minute. 'Diana Prince. As in Wonder Woman, from the comics?'

Paddy nodded. 'That little piggy is a trailblazer, a natural born leader. The others follow her every move.'

Finn twitched impatiently. 'Let's cut to the chase here, Paddy my man. What exactly do you want the dosh for?'

'Pet hotel.'

Finn snorted. 'Ha.'

I glanced at Paddy and he wasn't laughing. He was staring at the pigs.

I copped it. 'You mean a boarding kennel, like for dogs and cats?'

'Bingo.'

I looked around. 'Can you not keep them here?'

Paddy shook his head furiously. 'I need somewhere safe to keep 'em while I work on their tricks.'

'Safe. Why? Are they worth something?'

'Trust me, once I start uploading these videos, they'll be priceless.'

We followed Paddy's gaze over to the snoozing piglets.

'It'll be a digital epidemic,' Paddy said, matter-of-factly. 'Total disruption.'

I didn't doubt it. Paddy had his finger on the pulse. Everybody wanted a piece of the Paddy magic, hence the queue of people lining his basement.

Paddy blew his whistle suddenly, opening the gate of the pen. The pigs leapt up.

Finn shuffled. 'What the –?'

All six piglets had scurried over, surrounding Finn.

'Got yourself some fans, there, Finn,' I called out over the grunting, as the piglets sniffed at Finn's feet.

I turned to Paddy. 'Where'd you get them anyway?'

'Bought them off some aul' lad that my da knows. They were the runts of the litter.'

'The runts. No wonder they feel so comfortable with you, Finn,' I said, cackling, watching Finn hop from foot to foot.

'Very funny,' Finn said huffily.

Paddy picked up a filthy bucket and handed it to Finn. 'Here, they look thirsty.'

Finn flinched. 'Nah, you're all right, Paddy. These are new trainers, mate.'

'They'll go back in the pen if you fill up their water.'

While Finn battled with the bucket, I took the opportunity to get to the bottom of something that had been niggling me. 'All those people in your basement, Paddy. They'll pay you to plug their videos, surely?'

'Yeah, but it's a slow burner, Luke. Y'know these music types – it takes forever to get money from them. Too busy buskin' in town for pennies and tellin' themselves how fan-tab-ul-ous they are.'

I raised an eyebrow.

'Nah, my most lucrative business comes from girls and their face paint, believe it or not,' said Paddy.

It took me a minute to get it. 'Make-up?'

Paddy nodded. 'Plug a video on how to get the perfect

threaded eyebrow, or how to get rid of a giant zit in the middle of your forehead, and you're onto a winner. I've collaborated with a few girls and it's been very profitable.'

'Whoa, really?' I said, wondering what a threaded eyebrow was.

'You need to get online more, Luke,' Paddy murmured, as if reading my thoughts.

If only you knew, I thought, picturing the hard toilet seat.

'What about all the money you made from the Cedric videos?' I said, pressing my point.

Paddy pointed back towards the house. 'Reinvested it. Paid for that fancy editing equipment in there. Expensive piece of kit.'

I could well believe it.

'So I need a ball of cash to pay for the boarding kennel upfront,' said Paddy. 'Somewhere decent, too, not a kip. I want them to be well looked after.'

Finn approached us, kicking the gravel to dislodge the cakes of muck off his shoes. 'Right, Paddy, bro-talk. Let's get down to business. We're after a piece of the action – a slice of the pie, a … a … an aul' shlurp of the fizzy orange, get me?'

Paddy shot Finn a bemused look.

I raised an eyebrow. 'Smooth, Finn, smooth.'

I put my hand on Paddy's shoulder and got straight to the point. 'What Finn means is that we'd be looking for an investment offer, Paddy, as a trade-off for the loan. Still interested?'

Paddy threw us a double thumbs-up. 'I'm offering you a percentage of any earnings I make on the videos. Say, twenty per cent.'

'Thirty,' said Finn automatically.

Paddy countered. 'Twenty-five.'

The pigs had escaped the enclosure and were heading in Finn's direction again. He shot out his hand. 'Paddy, you've got yourself a deal.'

9

CROWD SURFING

I ducked out of the way of a schoolbag flying overhead.

Finn stopped, gazing around the dark, heaving room. 'Unbelievable. Flippin' unbelievable.'

We battled our way further into the crowd.

'This is off the scale.'

I nodded. 'They've totally nailed it.'

'How?' said Finn, bemused. 'They're not exactly mega-popular.'

I shrugged. 'The email?'

We'd all received this mysterious email from the Hunger Twins, instructing us to go to the school library at 8.30 AM.

'Ah, there you are.' We rotated on the spot to catch sight of Koby being airlifted towards us by swaying bodies. 'Welcome to the launch.'

Finn shook his head. 'How'd they pull this off?'

Koby beamed. 'Well, you know that Jo and Lucy announced the Tagged app a few weeks back, way ahead of the launch today. That generated a lot of interest.'

'Watch it, mate,' said Finn, as he narrowly avoided being trampled on by some oversized first-year.

'Why is everyone scrambling to get up there, though?' I said, pointing up to the top of the room where the Hunger Twins had set up camp.

'Because the first twenty people in the door today get the app free for life,' said Koby. 'A special launch promotion.'

'All the first- and second-years must be in here,' Finn exclaimed.

'And a few thirds.'

Finn's face lit up, like he was visualising a jackpot win on the slot machines. 'Bloody hell, I didn't think any third-years would be interested in it.'

I laughed. 'Poor Powder is on late duty this morning at the main gate. He looks really confused. Can't figure out why most of the school is in so early.'

Finn grunted. 'Disappointed his late-detention tally is so low, more like.'

I glanced at the door. 'I'm surprised we've not been busted.'

'Not yet,' said Finn.

'The noise levels in here are pretty high.'

Koby put his hand up. 'No, all the teachers are at some special "high-priority" meeting in the staffroom.'

'Come to think of it, Powder was looking very dapper this morning. He had his Conor McGregor special on.'

'The grey and pink pinstriped? Nice,' said Finn, chuckling.

Koby cut across us. 'Anyway, that's why we're having the launch at this insane time.' As dedicated as he was, even Koby loved his bed in the mornings.

Finn wagged his finger in approval. 'And right at the other end of the building. Clever.'

'Exactly. As far away from the staffroom as possible.'

I slapped him on the back. 'Good thinking, Kob.'

Up front, people started banging on the desks.

I stood up on my tiptoes. I could see Jo on her feet.

'Speech.'

'Speech.'

'Speech.'

A hush spread over the room.

'Eh, thanks everyone,' Jo stuttered. 'From today, the Tagged app is officially available for download.'

Cue some loud cheers.

Jo smiled, relaxing into it. 'Some lucky people who got here first today have got the app for free.'

More cheers.

I turned to Koby, impressed. 'She's not half-bad.'

Koby stretched up for a better look. 'I don't think she planned to say anything, you know.'

Jo picked up her phone. 'And we already have some tags. I can tell you that the first two people ever to be tagged are … Drumroll, please …'

Followed by another few bangs on the desk.

'Gabe O'Rourke and Matilda Brennan.'

'Matilda Brennan.' Finn smirked. 'Seriously? Gabe'd eat her for breakfast. She's a mouse.'

The whole room erupted. Two arms shot up from the middle of the room, complete with jazz hands.

I raised my eyebrows, recognising those gangly limbs immediately. 'Uh-oh.'

Swiftly, Gabe's body was launched up above everyone's head. He let out a rip-roaring yell, grinning wildly. He was passed up to the front, body-surfing the crowd.

Inevitably, the chanting started.

'Gabe.'

'Gabe.'

'Gabe.'

From the other corner of the room, there was a loud scream.

Poor Matilda Brennan never stood a chance. She was hoisted up into the air like a beach ball. Within seconds, they were bumping her up high and down towards the floor repeatedly.

'Tilda.'

'Tilda.'

'Tilda.'

Just then, the fluorescent lights flickered on all around the room.

A thunderous Powder Keane appeared at the door. 'What on earth is going on in here?' He forced his way through, followed by a group of curious, well-heeled visitors, one carrying a large TV camera on his shoulder.

Powder went on a rampage. 'PUT HER DOWN!'

The crowd released Matilda Brennan, who flopped to the floor with a thud.

'Everybody out of here, *now*,' said Powder, as the room fell silent. 'Get to class.'

He breathed in deeply, smoothed down his suit and turned to the visitors, all apologies. 'Please wipe this from your memory. Our students are normally much better behaved.'

A stylish lady in enormous high heels, who seemed to be the leader of the group, stepped forward. 'Mr Keane, this is awesome. Just awesome. In fact, this is exactly what we're looking for,' she drawled in a husky voice, with a distinct American twang.

Powder frowned. 'Ms Callaghan –'

She raised her hand. 'Please, call me Candice.'

'Ms Callaghan, this kind of thing is a once-off, believe me. It won't happen again.'

From where I was standing, I could almost hear Powder's jaw clenching.

Candice opened her mouth to speak, but Powder was on a roll.

'Here at St Patrick's Community College, we are a very run-of-the-mill school. No excitement. No theatrics. Just rules to be obeyed, lessons to be taught and exams to be sat. A well-oiled machine, as we like to say. So if it's drama you are looking for, then I'm afraid you've come to the wrong school for your fly-on-the-wall documentary.'

He was interrupted by Matilda Brennan, who emitted a ferocious groan, followed by a strange whimper. She clambered to her feet unsteadily, her face white with dizziness, her eyes rolling around in their sockets.

Then she vomited all over the library floor.

Multiple times.

The TV lady clapped her hands in glee. Then, remembering herself, hid her hands and cried: 'That poor child, somebody help her.'

Just then, Gabe, who'd been jostled onto the lads' shoulders, was catapulted upwards like a jet airliner. He landed smoothly, arms outstretched, but, unfortunately for Gabe, he didn't stop. He glided across the floor, hurtling perilously towards the pool of vomit.

I could barely watch. I covered my face with my hands and peered out through the slits between my fingers, praying that Gabe's brain was switched on, for once. Gabe was milliseconds away from a fate worse than anything Powder could ever dish out.

The whole room breathed in sharply, united in a simultaneous cringe.

With his nose practically in tipping distance of the contents of Matilda Brennan's stomach, Gabe sprang up on one hand, cartwheeled over the vomit and landed on two feet beside Candice, throwing her a cheeky wink.

The room erupted into applause.

Gabe bowed a few times. Like a hero.

Powder nearly lost it.

Nearly.

Only he had visitors.

The room evacuated at double speed.

And the cleaner was called.

'So, Matilda and Gabe. Probably not a runner,' Finn said, smirking, as he pushed past me and legged it up the corridor.

'I'm sure Gabe'll be heartbroken,' I shouted.

As I was edging my way out, I felt a tap on my shoulder.

Jo stared down at me, her eyes sparkling. 'Tagged. Over one hundred sold already.'

I glanced at my watch. 'But it's been in the app store for less than an hour.'

'This is just the start.' She strolled off, looking pleased.

I didn't move, just watched her tall shadow floating across the floor as I processed this information. We'd just made fifty quid in the last hour. Standing around. Doing nothing. Nothing at all. By the end of the day, we could be into the hundreds. By the end of the week, who knows?

A disturbing thought occurred to me. I wondered had Finn stumbled onto something golden after all.

Maybe this *was* easy money.

'Oi, Luke Morrissey.'

I swung around. A basketball came flying in the direction of my face, grazing my nose. Stumbling backwards, I was immediately cornered by a trio of lanky third-years wearing tank tops and long shorts, dripping sweat.

The tallest guy grabbed the ball back, spinning it on his index finger, eyeballing me all the while.

'Yeah,' I muttered uneasily, feeling the heat.

Another one gripped my wrist and flipped over my hand. They each slapped money into my palm.

'Three saving specials, bud.'

I stared at the spinning ball, momentarily disorientated.

One prodded me. 'You listening? Three Gabe O'Rourke's saving specials.'

I blinked, closing my palm tightly.

Word of Gabe's savings scheme was spreading.

As far as the basketball team anyway.

10

THE DARK BISHOP

I checked my phone. One missed call from Finn. I tried to concentrate on walking fast, but my mind kept wandering back to the blank TV screen. I had flicked on the TV to catch the big derby match, only to be faced with a black void.

Channel unavailable.

Subscription cancelled.

Things must be tight at home if Dad was forced to cancel the sports, considering he spends most days and nights staring at golf repeats. Not that the parents have come clean to me about how bad things are. But the Arctic undercurrent in the house was getting chillier by the minute. I wondered if this bank idea would net us some really serious cash. That sports package didn't come cheap.

I heard Finn call out. 'Take your time, Lukey, no rush.'

I realised that I had slowed to a snail's pace.

'C'mon, Mucker's gaff is down here,' said Finn, leading the way. 'You see the derby last night? What a cracker.'

I half-nodded.

$ $ $

Mucker McGrath stood at the gate dressed entirely in black. We only knew he was there because of the light from his phone screen.

He looked past us. 'Anyone else know you're here?

'No.'

'You sure? Nobody followed you?'

'No. Feck sake, Mucker. What's with all the secrecy? This isn't a meeting of the mafia brotherhood.'

I shivered. 'Can we go inside?'

'This way.'

We followed Mucker through the side gate, down the narrow alley and across to the shed at the bottom of his garden.

Mucker stopped at the shed door. 'Now, this is just between us, lads. Not a word to anybody. Nobody.'

We both nodded, eager to get out of the cold.

I squeezed past him into the shed, which was packed high with large brown boxes.

Finn glanced around. 'What's with all the boxes, Mucker?'

'Stock.'

Finn raised an eyebrow at me.

I peeked inside one. 'Shoes?'

Mucker reached in and pulled out a plain white shoebox. He threw it at me. 'Take a look.'

I opened it and let out a small yelp.

'Bloody hell! They're the new Ronaldos,' said Finn, making a grab for the football boots.

'Top of the range,' said Mucker softly.

'Just like Speedy's new ones,' I murmured.

'Yeah,' Finn said, running his fingers along the boot. Then he looked up, frowning. 'Hold on. Speedy told me he bought his boots from the Dark Bishop. I was convinced they were fakes.'

Mucker said nothing.

Finn's eyes widened like saucers. 'No way.'

Still Mucker said nothing.

'No feckin' way. You're kidding me,' said Finn breathlessly.

Mucker's nose twitched.

Finn banged the soles of the two boots together with a clatter. 'Mucker McGrath. Are you tryin' to tell us that you're the Dark Bishop? Legendary underground supplier of all the latest sports gear –'

'At the cheapest prices,' I finished.

'Pull the other one,' said Finn, unconvinced.

'Not possible,' I said, doing the maths. 'The Dark Bishop has been around too long.'

Mucker popped a piece of gum in his mouth. 'Inherited the business from the brother, Timmy, when he went off to college. He still gets his cut, of course.'

Finn looked up. 'Timmy. You mean *the* Mucker McGrath?'

'The original,' said Mucker.

Mucker had also inherited his nickname from his older brother Timmy, who was forever known as Mucker McGrath since he'd turned up in school wearing his foul-smelling cattle-chasing wellies. Word has it the stench was so stomach-turning it even had Powder lost for words as he came up for air. Timmy was a rough diamond, by all accounts.

Younger Mucker's feet were also a topic of interest. Personally, I'd not experienced it first hand, but I gathered that he was also afflicted with the same foot odour issues as his older brother, so the nickname stuck.

Finn examined the boots closely, scraping at the designer logo. Mucker watched him. 'Lads, they're not fakes.'

'They're knock offs then,' Finn said, dropping the boots back into the box like they were burning his fingers.

I stared at Mucker, taking in his tall, skinny frame, dangly arms, spiky ginger hair, round freckly face and thick-rimmed glasses. Not your average dodgy goods dealer.

Mucker shook his head fiercely. 'Not stolen. They're promotional goods.'

'Ah-ha, they're second-hand,' said Finn, clicking his fingers at Mucker.

'No, no, lads,' said Mucker, becoming slightly agitated from the interrogation. 'Well, OK, technically speaking, they're not new. One previous owner, unused.'

'Can't you just tell us where you pick all this gear up from?' I said, still doubtful.

'Lukey's right, Mucker lad,' Finn said. 'Spit it out.'

'I've a contact on the inside. My uncle works as a sports-gear agent. He gets me all the gear at discount prices,' Mucker admitted, finally.

Finn leaned against a box, shaking his head. 'Flippin' hell, Mucker. I dunno what to say. You're a dark horse, mate.'

'A dark bishop,' I threw in.

Was it any wonder Mucker was a no-show at school most days, juggling this business empire behind the scenes?

Finn scrunched up his face. 'Yeah, what's with the weird name? It's like something out of *Lord of the Rings*.'

Mucker looked at us like it was obvious. 'The bishop that only moves on the dark squares.'

Finn and I exchanged glances. Neither of us had a clue.

'You don't play chess then,' said Mucker. 'It's a chess term. The bishop, like, the chess piece.'

'You got me, Mucker. Board games aren't really my thing.'

Mucker made a face. 'Board game. No way. Chess is life, Finn boy. Chess is life.'

Another surprise. Mucker and chess were not an obvious match.

A sharp wind blew straight through the shed. I rubbed my hands together and pulled my woolly hat further down over my ears. 'So, what exactly are we doin' here, Mucker?' I said, hoping we could veer the conversation towards the actual point of our visit.

Mucker pushed his glasses in tight against his nose. 'I've an opportunity in the pipeline.'

Finn's eyes gleamed. 'Good stuff, Mucker. We luurrve a good opportunity.'

'Let him speak, Finn,' I cut in, before anyone jumped the gun.

'I spoke to my uncle last night. He's got a scorcher that will really sell. Has to close this week, though. So I need to lay my hands on some cash, quick.'

'Aren't you rakin' it in here with these boots?' I said quickly. I knew at least half our soccer club were wearing them. And at our game at the weekend, the goalie on the opposite team was boasting about ordering them. Mucker's boots were the grand slam of boots right now.

'Bad timing. Lots of stock right now and not enough cash.'

'How much d'you need?' I said.

'Two hundred and fifty.'

Finn puffed out his cheeks. 'Jeez, Mucker. Two-fifty.'

'What's the deal?' I said, ignoring Finn's dramatics.

Mucker made a face. 'Can't say. Sworn to secrecy.'

Finn laughed. 'Wha'? Mucker, you can't expect us to hand over cash in the dark, man.'

'My lips are sealed. You'll have to trust me. I swear it'll be worth your while.'

I sat back, shifting my eyes over the contents of the shed, counting quickly. As I suspected, Mucker was sitting on hundreds.

Finn stretched out his hands, a toothy smirk spreading over his face. 'Make me an offer I can't refuse, Mucker boy.'

Mucker chewed carefully. 'What's the interest on your loans?'

'Twenty per cent,' Finn replied immediately.

'I'm willing to pay twenty-five. For your silence.'

'Done.'

'And a pair of boots each,' I threw in.

'Sound.'

Mucker put out his hand.

Finn looked at me. I nodded. We shook on it. Mucker was good for the cash. He was a solid investment. Koby would be proud.

Plus a decent pair of boots. Happy days.

Finn whistled. 'Still can't believe it. Gentle giant Mucker McGrath – the Dark Bishop.'

Mucker raised his eyebrows. 'Keep a lid on it, lads, won't ya? Don't want to ruin my mobster reputation.'

A thought occurred to me. I replayed our conversation in the butcher's shop about outstanding loans in my head. 'Why did you take out a loan for one pair of rugby boots from us, Mucker? I mean, c'mon, you're surrounded by boots.'

'Just testin' the water. Wanted to see if you were the real deal,' said Mucker, cocking his head towards Finn, smirking. 'You never know, with this fella involved.'

'Wise guy,' said Finn, in his best Italian mobster imitation, air-punching Mucker's shoulder.

'By the way, how'd you hear about our bank?' I said, curious.

'Chess.'

'Huh?'

'I'm in the youth club with Lucy Sullivan. We play chess.'

I was impressed.

No need to advertise. Word was out.

11

THE STABBING

Mr Rafferty strode into the classroom, all business. 'Quiet, please.'

The murmuring continued.

He pointed towards the TV crew, squished in the corner. 'OK, OK, I know it's exciting to have TV cameras in the classroom, but you need to pretend they are not there. Act as normal.'

'Is that a shirt you're wearin', sir?'

'Lookin' very dapper.'

'Is your usual grey hoodie in the wash, sir?'

'He's makin' an effort for the cameras.'

'Hopin' for a new career on the big screen, aren't ya, sir?'

'Bought a new shirt an' all for it.'

There were fits of laughter.

'All right, pipe down. Get out your books and turn to chapter seven: Marketing.'

This request was met by a series of loud grunts.

'More marketing.'

'Marketing again, sir?'

'Today we are going to tackle something more interesting: online marketing.'

More grunts.

Mr Rafferty scribbled the word 'viral' on the board.

There was a tap on the door.

'Yes?'

Paddy Tarantino's face appeared around the door. 'Sir.'

'Paddy, great. Come on in.' Mr Rafferty cleared his throat. 'Today we are going to talk about viral Internet campaigns. And to kick things off, Paddy's going to show us some of his cat videos that have gone viral. Can anybody tell me what the word "viral" means?'

'Is it the smell from Mucker McGrath's shoes, sir?'

'He said "viral", not vile.'

Everyone erupted into laughter.

'OK, settle down. Viral marketing is when information and opinions about a product or service are spread electronically from one Internet user to another.'

'Like the flu, sir,' Podge Egan piped up.

Mr Rafferty frowned. 'Sort of. Go ahead and set up, Paddy.'

Paddy opened his laptop.

'OK. Examples, please. Can anyone give me an example of something that's gone viral online?'

'Mona Lisa Murphy knows all about going viral, sir.'

Annalisa Murphy went pink.

Mr Rafferty bellowed, 'Enough.'

Podge Egan's hand flew up. 'Paddy's cat videos, sir. They went viral.'

The class groaned.

'Podge, you plank.'

'Podge, spot on, as usual.'

Mr Rafferty sighed. 'Engage brain, Mr Egan. I just told you that. An example other than Paddy, please.'

'Ugh, sir, sir, make it stop!' Emily hopped out of her chair at the back of the class and pointed to Gabe, who was snoring, his head resting on the edge of her desk.

Mr Rafferty breathed out loudly, teeth gritted. He walked to the back of the room, pulling out his phone. He shoved it beside Gabe's ear and let off the alarm at top volume.

Gabe sprang up in his chair, stunned.

'Ah, Mr O'Rourke. Welcome back. Next time I have to wake you up in class, you're in detention.'

Gabe blinked, wiping the drool from his chin.

'Come on, folks. One example is all I'm asking for,' said Mr Rafferty.

'Twinkle Twinks,' said Emily. 'The beauty blogger. She gets trillions of hits.'

Mr Rafferty spun around. 'Good, Emily. Go on.'

'Well, her video on eyelash tinting went viral.'

'Eyelash tinting, OK,' said Mr Rafferty, struggling.

'And her blog on eyebrow threading, it was revolutionary,' Emily added. The rest of the girls murmured their agreement.

Eyebrow threading again. I glanced over at Paddy, who winked knowingly at me.

Mr Rafferty rubbed his own eyebrows self-consciously. 'Erm, right. Nice example, Emily. Anyone else got anything?'

Gabe leapt to his feet, yanking his bike helmet on. 'Luke, I am your father.'

Everyone sniggered.

'Luke, I am your father,' Gabe boomed.

'Gabe, sit.'

'He's talkin' about *Star Wars*, sir. The new *Star Wars* film,' Finn interpreted.

Mr Rafferty didn't react at first, just observed Gabe as he reefed the helmet off, grinned widely, and collapsed back down.

'Yes, yes, you're right. The film preview went viral,' Mr Rafferty said slowly.

'Boom,' said Finn.

'Wow,' said Mr Rafferty, shaking his head in surprise. 'I can't believe I'm going to say this, but … good contribution, Gabe.'

Gabe didn't react. He had zoned out again.

Mr Rafferty turned to the projector. 'Right, I think we'd better take a look at these videos. What are you going to show us first, Paddy?'

Paddy started into his customary speech with his usual over-enthusiasm. The class was distracted, though. Some sort of commotion was brewing right outside. Paddy was really getting stuck into it when there was a loud shriek, followed by a series of snappy barks.

Suddenly, Paddy's face dropped. He ran over and pulled open the door. 'Oh, no!'

'What is it?' said Mr Rafferty, following him out.

'It's my pigs, sir. I think they've escaped.'

'Your what?'

It transpired the climax of Paddy's marketing 'lesson' was a sneak preview of his soon-to-be-celebrity marching piglet troop. He'd paraded the pigs into school and tied them to the water fountain in the locker area outside the classroom.

I hopped out of my seat to get a better look. The cameraman from the TV crew wasn't far behind me, almost tripping over himself to capture the unfolding drama.

'Sir, get that yoke outta there, its ruinin' me brand-new coat,' screamed a traumatised first-year, pointing at one piglet happily snoozing in her ground-floor locker.

Unfortunately for Mr Rafferty, he was the first teacher at the scene and was forced to confront the chaos alone.

'Sir, they stink.'

'Feck sake. They've scoffed me lunch, sir.'

'Sir, one's after pooing behind the plant.'

The other piglets were tucked in the corner outside the woodwork classroom, grazing on the spewed contents of some lunchboxes.

'Paddy, do something,' said Mr Rafferty, desperation creeping in.

Paddy scrambled for his whistle and blew it loudly.

The pigs shuffled up half-heartedly, snouts still mooching at the food.

'Ah, now the fun really starts. Here's Powder,' said Finn, nodding towards a bulky figure storming up the corridor. 'Right on cue.'

Just at that moment, the door to the woodwork room flew open. Tank, the school caretaker, bungled out, holding a large screwdriver. He tripped over the first piglet and collapsed on top of the second, the screwdriver piercing the piglet straight through the leg.

The piglet let out a painful bark.

Cursing, Tank scrambled to his feet, the bloodied weapon still in hand.

The girls recoiled in horror.

Paddy raced over, hysterical.

'What on earth?' Powder's voice bellowed.

'Ho-ho,' said Finn gleefully, 'it's total carnage.'

Powder quickened his pace.

The TV crew made a beeline for him, sticking the camera directly in Powder's face.

'Get that thing out of my way.' Powder made a grab for the camera, lost his balance and fell flat on his back into a neat mound of sticky pig dung.

Finn rubbed his hands gleefully. 'What a day! This just gets better and better.'

'I don't know what you're looking so pleased about.'

We turned to see Emily tapping her foot.

She nodded towards the chaos. 'That's Diana Prince.'

Finn narrowed his eyes. 'Who?'

'The pig over there, spilling blood and guts. That's Diana Prince. Our star piggy.'

We all looked at each other blankly.

She slapped her forehead, frustrated. 'You guys are thick sometimes. She's the lead piggy, the one that all the other little piggies follow and copy. Without her …'

An image of the pigs marching about in Paddy's yard popped into my head, with Diana Prince at the helm. Suddenly, I copped it. Diana Prince was the glue that held this little piggy troop together. Without her, it was like having a team with no captain. 'Damn. You mean, no Diana Prince then, potentially, no marching pigs?'

'Uh-huh, meaning …?' Emily said encouragingly.

I winced. 'Meaning, no pig videos?'

Finn emitted a sharp cry, probably visualising all that potential profit, zapped. 'No pig videos.'

Emily rolled her eyes. 'Finally, they get it.'

12
THE PROMO

'Mr Fitzpatrick. To what do I owe the pleasure?'

Finn smiled down at Miss Shine, all innocent. 'Wha', Miss? I'm here to audition for the musical.'

Miss Shine shooed him into line.

'Right, listen up, everyone. Margie is going to play "Food, Glorious Food". Please sing at the tops of your voices. Loud and proud, so I can hear you. The lyrics are written up there on the board.'

She nodded at Margie, who started on the piano.

'Remember, loud and proud.'

As we sang, Miss Shine paraded up the row, like a drill sergeant inspecting her platoon. She stopped occasionally, rising onto her toes and perking her ear, scrutinising every note. As she got closer, I could feel my voice begin to quiver. Beside me, little Bobby McDonagh was squawking like a duck. But she sailed past us as if we weren't even there.

When she got to Finn, she stopped dead. Finn puffed out his chest and cranked the volume up until he was practically shouting.

But Miss Shine had her poker face on. When she reached

the end of the line, she spun on her high heels and clapped her hands. Margie stopped playing.

'Not bad. Let's go again. Anybody that I tap on the shoulder, please stop singing.'

She walked behind the line this time, blindside, just to really mess with our heads. I peeked over my shoulder. As Miss Shine approached Finn, her face twisted and distorted, as if she'd got brain-freeze. Finn, sensing her presence, turned the volume up another notch, belting out the song in his best Cockney accent. Miss Shine reacted like she'd been scarred for life. She couldn't tap Finn's shoulder fast enough.

I turned back around and kept singing.

Tap.

'You, please.' I felt her hand on my shoulder.

Tap.

'And you, Bobby.'

Bobby McDonagh – the squawking duck – was out too.

Tap.

Tap.

Tap.

Her face finally relaxed. 'OK, now, that sounds better.'

She clapped her hands again. The hall went quiet.

'Anyone that is singing, congratulations – you made the chorus line. Anyone that isn't, you can be in the chorus, but I'm afraid you need to mime.'

'Mime,' said Finn, genuinely horrified. 'But, Miss, that's total mortification.'

Miss Shine glared at him. 'A miming orphan in the workhouse scene in the opening act. That's my only offer.'

'But, Miss, being an ex-model, I've got experience –'

There were muffled laughs from the line.

'Plus I auditioned for that reality singing competition on TV.'

Miss Shine's eyebrows shot up. She removed her glasses and shot Finn a look of bemusement. 'Really? And did you progress?'

Finn sighed. 'Well, no.'

There was a loud snort, followed by a stream of fake laughter. 'Ask him what the judges said, Miss.'

I swung around.

The crowd parted to reveal Kimberley Farrell, ready to pounce.

Kim 'Chip on My Shoulder' Farrell. One of Finn's most infamous casualties. He'd ceremoniously ditched her over loudspeaker on cup-final day in first year, and she'd been out to cripple him ever since.

Miss Shine peered down the hall. 'Kimberley, what's so funny?'

'The judges ... er ... I was just remembering what the judges said to him, Miss,' Kimberley spluttered, play-acting. 'What was it again, Fitzpatrick? Wailing foxes?'

Miss Shine turned to Finn and crossed her arms. 'Please, we'd all love to hear what the judges said.'

Finn rolled his shoulders uncomfortably.

'Mr Fitzpatrick?'

Finn stared straight ahead.

'It's on the Internet, Miss,' Kimberley added with a smirk, reaching for her phone.

'All right, all right,' said Finn, hunched. 'They said I sounded like a cross between teenage girls wailing over the break-up of the latest boy band and foxes fighting over a dead cat.'

Miss Shine smirked. 'Case closed.'

In the line, the muffled laughs turned into hysterics.

'I'm afraid it's a "No" from me.' She pointed at me. 'To both of you. Scoot. Now.'

'But, Miss, I'm happy to mime,' I protested.

Miss Shine raised her hand. 'No, this musical is a serious business. There's no room for any messing.'

I didn't bother objecting. Out of the corner of my eye, I saw Koby signalling madly to us from the side of the hall, and slouched over.

'What are you guys doing here?' Koby asked with a quizzical face, scanning the room.

I nudged him. 'C'mon Kob, the school musical. Guaranteed two hours off class a week.'

'Even more in the run-up to opening night. And we've blown it,' Finn moaned. 'Bloody Kimberly Farrell and her motor mouth.'

I bit my lip. 'So nothing to do with your singing, then?'

'Well, I've got something that'll cheer you up,' said Koby. He handed us both a recycled crisp packet, eyes shining. 'It's our first payout. Don't open it here.'

Finn perked up. 'How much?'

'Seventy-five.'

'Nice.' I'd nearly made my initial investment back.

Finn snorted. 'Peanuts.'

'C'mon Finn, it's a decent start.'

Koby nodded. 'Yeah, keep calm, Finn, keep calm.'

'We need to put our foot down on the pedal. Get in some hard hitters. Especially if Paddy's pigs are going to nosedive.'

Koby stared at Finn. 'Haven't you heard?'

'Heard what?'

'About the pigs?'

Finn's face fell. 'Don't tell me. They're mincemeat?'

'Bacon?' I threw in.

Koby shook his head. 'No, lads, listen. You know the way the TV crew filmed the whole "piglets wreak havoc in school" incident?'

We nodded.

Koby's voice quivered with excitement. 'They used it as a promo for their fly-on-the-wall documentary. It was uploaded last night and it's trending today. It's all over the Internet. And guess who's the star of the show?'

'Powder?'

'Nope, Diana Prince, of course. Our limping piglet.'

Finn's mouth dropped. 'No way. Champion!'

'Powder's coming in a close second, by the way.'

I rolled my eyes. 'Surprise, surprise. The TV crew got some quality footage of Powder slipping and sliding around in the pig slop.'

'And one of his classic rants afterwards,' said Koby.

I took out my phone to log on. 'So what else have we missed?'

'Well, after the promo went live, Paddy put up a video showing how Diana Prince was recovering from her stabbing ordeal. She was dragging her little bandaged hoof across the floor. People are loving her.'

I wrinkled my nose. 'Who'd have thought a three-legged piglet would become such a hero?'

'She's building up quite a core following. Paddy could dedicate a whole online channel to her at this rate.'

'Paddy must've known that bringin' those pigs into the school building was a risk,' I said thoughtfully.

'It paid off,' said Koby. 'Maybe he was hoping for a bit of drama.'

'He hadn't planned on the stabbing, of course,' said Finn. 'That was an unexpected bonus.'

'Hardly. He loves those pigs.'

'You had me worried, Kob. I was sure the pigs investment had flatlined.' Finn stuck out his tongue. 'That little piggy could double our profits overnight. Everyone's a winner.'

'Well, except for Mr Rafferty. I'm sure the backlash from Powder was rough.'

'Ha. Raffo was showing off in front of the cameras.'

I looked up at Finn. 'You think?'

'Totally. There's no way he'd have brought Paddy in doing that presentation if the TV crowd weren't around. He got stung, for once.'

'Nah, he's too intelligent for that.'

'Trust me. It's not enough that he's a Z-list radio celebrity. He's set his sights on TV domination now.'

Mr Rafferty later grudgingly admitted to our business studies class that the whole three-legged-pig episode was an impressive example of viral marketing. He also let slip that he was forced to sit through repeated verbal bombings from Powder on the topic of his much-loved, now forever-ruined, pig-stained, pale-blue suit.

13

LOCHY MULGREW

'What's so funny?' I leapt into the huddle of sniggering girls, who all screeched and immediately hid their phones behind their backs.

'What's up with them?' I said, wandering over to the lads sitting at a canteen table.

'It's that Tagged app. They are all completely obsessed with it.' Pablo grunted noisily.

Finn grabbed Pablo in a headlock and ruffled his hair. 'Poor Pablo. Harassed, he was. Got tagged so many times he's had to remove his profile altogether.'

'It was driving me crazy, man,' said Pablo, shaking Finn off. 'They are like a pack of wolves, these women, surrounding me.'

I laughed. Pablo wasn't getting any sympathy from me, the handsome fecker.

'I didn't realise Tagged was such a success,' I said, turning to Finn, hoping to rub it in.

He was too busy texting on his phone to notice.

'It's so unbelievable, man,' Pablo responded instead. 'Almost everyone in the school has downloaded it.'

'You serious?'

Pablo looked at me. 'You're not on it?'

I shook my head. After my failed attempt to create a profile, I'd given up. Anyway, it wasn't really my thing.

'Take my advice. Don't go there, man.'

Finn glanced up. 'Ha. Lukey won't have the same problems as you, Pablo. He's not exactly Ronaldo.'

I puffed out my chest, winking. 'Not even with this buff bod?'

Truth was, after the launch of the app, I hadn't really been tracking its progress. I'd left that in Koby's hands. I shook my head and made a mental note to get on to Koby to see exactly what Tagged had produced in the way of profit.

I elbowed Finn. 'Who're you texting?'

'Wouldn't you like to know, Lukey boy.'

'Ah-ha, I bet it's a girl, a match on Tagged,' said Pablo, fluttering his eyelids.

I threw Finn a sideways glance, wondering was it on or off with Finn and Caterina at the moment.

'It's ON, before you even ask,' Finn quickly confirmed, glaring at Pablo. 'Don't be starting rumours.'

But Pablo had already jumped up and was heading towards the canteen queue.

'Is that a new phone?'

Finn nodded coyly. 'I upgraded.'

I grabbed it. 'Jeez, Finn. That's the latest android. It's worth –'

'Yeah, OK, OK,' Finn replied hotly. 'Thought I'd treat myself.'

I whistled. 'Splashing the cash already.'

Finn grinned. 'Why not? It'll be rollin' in soon, Lukey. Everything we touch turns to gold.'

He had a point. We seemed to be on a roll.

Finn took the phone back. 'Actually, if you must know, it's

Lochy Mulgrew on the text,' he whispered, showing me the screen. 'He needs a loan to clear a payout.'

'Mulgrew.' I narrowed my eyes. Lochy Mulgrew ran the biggest, most lucrative betting book in the school. He'd run a bet on anything if he thought it would gather enough interest to turn him a healthy profit. My last encounter with him, I'd lost twenty quid betting on the annual Teachers vs Sixth-Year Students table quiz. Specialist subject: sport. Embarrassingly, the teachers ran away with it, showing up the current horde of sixth-years as a total bunch of melons.

'Lochy's sound out, but you know he's shifty as hell too, Finn. Total chancer. And he's from town, so we've no idea who he knocks around with.'

'Reckons he has a big ticket coming up,' said Finn, choosing to ignore my comments. 'Something juicy.'

I regarded Finn dubiously. 'What? A bet?'

'Doesn't say. He wants to meet to discuss.'

'Yo, yo.' Gabe appeared and plonked himself down opposite us. He produced a large rusted biscuit tin and took the lid off.

'What you up to?' I said, leaning over to look inside the tin. It was empty.

'Lunch,' said Gabe casually.

He dumped three large bags of salad leaves onto the table, opened each one and emptied them into the tin.

Finn poked the tin. 'What the hell is that?'

'Salad.'

Finn shook his head. 'I can see that, Gabe. Why are you eating a mountain of lettuce?'

'The coach said to eat more green veg.'

'Well you've a field full of the stuff there all right.'

'Problem is, I hate salad.'

'Now what are you doing?'

Gabe had taken his bottle of cheap, supermarket-brand, tooth-decaying cola and was splashing it liberally over the salad leaves. He slugged a mouthful of the cola, burped, grabbed his plastic fork and tucked in.

'Problem solved,' he said, beaming, green bits lodged between his teeth.

$ $ $

Lochy Mulgrew raised his hands dramatically. 'Speedy O' Neill verses Moses Obaya. Last man standing.'

Finn gasped. 'Obaya. The fifth-year?'

'Aye.'

'He's a flippin' rocket.'

'Aye.'

'Sprinting?'

'Ach, no. Bor-ing,' said Lochy, tutting.

'What, then?' said Finn impatiently.

Lochy's eyes shone. 'Penalty shootout, lads. The first to five penalties wins.'

I whistled.

'Obaya will win that hands down,' said Finn. 'He is, without a doubt, the best striker in the school. Actually, in the county.'

'I wouldn't be so sure, Finn,' Lochy said. 'It'll be a close call. What's your take, Luke? You're the one feeds the ball in to Speedy from midfield.'

I exhaled loudly. 'Speedy's on form. He's produced the goods in practically every game we've played lately. He must be catchin' Obaya's goal tally. Well, there can't be much between them.'

'True,' Finn said. 'But Obaya is such a quality finisher.'

'Speedy's finish has improved a lot this year, though,' I argued. 'He could set up camp down the pitch, he puts in so much practice.'

Finn punched the air. 'Bloody hell, Lochy. You've lined up a gem, so. Two best strikers in the school go head to head. Speedy versus Obaya.'

'Will Obaya agree to it?' Rumour was that he was a fairly serious individual. I doubted very much that he'd want to be associated with Lochy and his crew either.

Lochy smiled lazily, shaking out his scraggy hair. 'Not yet. That's where you boys come in, Luke. I need you to use all your charm on him.'

'Can't you do that?' I said, wondering why we needed to be involved.

Lochy hooted. 'Ach, Obaya won't even speak to me, thinks I'm a total waste of oxygen.'

Lochy leaned back and grabbed a chisel. We were standing at the back of the woodwork room, watching as he attempted to carve a groove into a muddled diagonal piece of wood.

'What's that you're making, Lochy mate?' Finn said, frowning.

'A wee footstool.'

'Really? It's a triangle, though.'

Lochy grinned. 'Aye, it's a work in progress.'

'So what about this loan?' I said.

'It's just small beans, lads. Need three hundred to cover a bet payout. Somebody got lucky. Always bad news for us bookies.'

'Three hundred.' I eyeballed Finn. This would be our largest loan to date.

Lochy spotted my face. 'Hey, I'm good for the cash, with this penalty shootout on the cards. I'll repay it, plus interest.'

'The finance is yours,' Finn said assuredly. 'We'll get Koby to do up the paperwork.'

'Whoa, whoa, we'll need to go over our figures first, Lochy,' I said, interjecting before Finn completely jumped the gun. 'We'll get back to you in the next few days.'

Finn glared at me, but I wasn't bothered.

'Ach, no problem, Luke. Don't take too long, though.'

'So this penalty contest – when and where?' I asked, changing the subject.

'Three weeks. After the cup match. Probably at the local pitch.'

'Sound.' I picked up the chisel and ran my finger along the edge. I still had doubts about getting involved – Lochy was an unknown. 'What's the deal then? If we get Obaya on board?'

'A cut of the profits on all bets placed on the shootout,' Lochy replied immediately.

Tidy sum, if everything fell into place. I glanced over at Finn, who danced a little celebratory jig behind Lochy's back.

Lochy stood back, admiring his handiwork. 'Will you guys be throwing down a wager?'

Finn rubbed his hands together. 'Absolutely, Lochy boy, ab-so-lute-ly. My money's on Obaya.'

I heard the faint sound of the bell ringing. I nudged Finn towards the door.

'By the way, lads, I've just opened a book on the ladies' junior hockey team, if you're interested?'

I made a face. 'Nah, let's go.'

Finn perked up. 'Hold on, what odds, Lochy?'

Lochy looked up from his footstool. 'Well, you know their next match is against St Marys, who have that machine Tonnes Toohy in defence. But, still in all, I'm giving our lot an even chance.'

'Who's on the team?' Finn asked.

Lochy listed out the names.

Finn smiled when he heard Katy Doyle's name. 'Ahhh, Luke's girlfriend.'

Lochy's eyes widened and he flicked a pencil stub in my direction. 'Nooo way. You kept that quiet, Morrissey, you wee animal. Fair play.'

I felt my face redden. 'She's not my girlfriend. I barely know the girl.'

'Soon-to-be girlfriend then,' Finn said, still digging, as he walked off, dragging me along by the arm. 'A work in progress.'

Lochy's eyebrows lifted. 'Aye, a bit like this stool, lads.'

'Big romance. Watch this space, Lochy,' Finn called back, tossing my hair.

'Aye, aye. I'll open a book on it, wha'?' shouted Lochy, grinning from ear to ear.

14

THE GOLDEN TICKETS

Mucker McGrath frowned. He fiddled furiously with the padlock on the back door. 'You sure it's secure? This gear is worth a lot of money.'

Finn waved the torch around the butcher's shop. 'Look around. No self-respecting thief would set foot in here.'

Mucker sniffed, running his hands along the brown boxes like they were his babies. He turned and threw Finn a wad of fifty-euro notes.

Finn handed the cash to me.

I passed it over to Koby, who started counting.

'Don't worry, Mucker,' said Finn, casually plonking himself down on the nearest box. 'The place has been empty, like, for ever. Nobody ever comes near it.'

Mucker relaxed a little. 'Thanks, lads. I couldn't have all the boxes hanging around, not with workmen crawling the house building this extension.'

'All square here,' Koby announced, nodding at Mucker and rolling the cash back up.

Mucker nodded. 'So what's the play when I need the gear back?'

'Just call me and I'll unlock the place for you, no hassle,' Finn replied easily.

Mucker shifted on his feet.

'You all right, Mucker?' I said, noticing his unease.

Silently, Mucker slipped his bag off his back and hauled out another shoe box. He removed the lid to reveal a brown envelope, stuffed with shimmering cards. He held a card out and Finn made a grab for it.

'Meet David Romero. Bloody hell, Luke. David Romero,' Finn spluttered, eyes dazzling, mouth salivating. 'Mucker, mate, these are pure gold.'

I looked over Finn's shoulder and read: 'Meet David Romero for a one-on-one session at Blood, Sweat and Tears sports shop –'

'Sweet, right?' Mucker interrupted.

I whistled. 'Hell, yeah. This guy was the highest-rated player in the Premier League last season. And he's bangin' the goals in already this season.'

'Totally. My points tally is off the charts,' said Finn proudly.

Mucker looked at Finn, confused.

'Fantasy football,' I explained.

Mucker nodded, still unsure.

'Not a Premier League man, then?' I said.

Mucker twitched. 'Nah, not my bag. I try to tune in a bit, just for business.'

'So Romero, he's definitely coming here?' I said doubtfully, glancing at the ticket again.

Mucker shrugged. 'Some promotional thing for Blood, Sweat and Tears.'

'How'd you get these?'

'The uncle. Thing is, I can't sell them for a few weeks, not until the event is officially announced. So I'm looking for somewhere safe to store them too.'

'Look no further, Mucker,' said Finn, arms outstretched.

Mucker whipped the ticket out of Finn's hand, uncertain.

Finn clicked his fingers. 'I've got it.'

He sprinted over to the grimy stainless-steel sink, clutched both ends of the basin, and, after a few tugs, dislodged it from its fittings.

Finn pointed inside the old water pipe. 'Hide the tickets in there.'

Mucker waggled his finger inside the top of the pipe to check if it was dry.

'There's no water. The pump's turned off,' Koby said, watching him.

Finn kicked the sink. 'Place is derelict. Nothin' in it works.'

Mucker dabbed his forehead thoughtfully. 'Can you guys keep the Romero thing under wraps?'

'Of course,' Finn said confidently.

I watched Mucker's face. I understood what he was really asking. Could we be trusted? Maybe he was worried we'd split with all his gear and the tickets.

I looked him straight in the eye. 'Don't worry, Mucker. We're good.'

He nodded, holding eye contact.

I placed my hand on Finn's shoulder. 'Well, whatever about this waster, you can trust myself and Kob anyway,' I said, lightening the mood.

Finn smirked. 'Funny.'

Mucker paused for a moment then rolled the brown envelope

up tight and stuffed it deep into the pipe. After a moment he stood back and nodded, allowing Finn to fit the sink back in place.

'So any chance of a ticket ourselves, Mucker? Seeing as we're doin' you this favour an' all?'

Mucker smiled lazily at Finn, like he'd been waiting for it. 'One ticket, and you can fight over it.'

$ $ $

'Not a word to Emily. Strictly between the three of us.'

I threw Finn a look.

'What? This storage arrangement with Mucker has nothin' to do with the bank,' he said defensively.

I waited for Koby's reaction, but he just shrugged and divided the money we'd got from Mucker in three, handing each of us a bundle.

I gripped his wrist. 'New watch, Kob?'

Koby's face lit up. 'Yeah, it's got a touch screen. Wanna see?'

He swiped through the different screens over-enthusiastically. 'Steep?'

Koby nodded. 'But worth it. Anyway we have to do something with all this cash, right?'

'Have your parents seen it?'

'I told them I got it in the discount shop.'

'And they actually believed that?'

Koby shrugged. 'What've you bought?'

'Nothing yet.'

'Nothing at all?' said Finn, incredulous.

I gnawed at my fingernails. 'It's called self-control, Finn.'

I wasn't sure what to do with the quantities of cash coming our way. We'd already got another bundle each from the bank. This time carefully wrapped in shiny gold wrappers. Nice touch, courtesy of Koby.

These little money piles were growing steadily under my mattress. Meanwhile, downstairs, the parents were skint. Hardly two beans to rub together. Mam was hoarding cheap tomato soup by the caseload, like a nuclear catastrophe was on the cards. I was half-expecting to unearth an underground survival bunker, filled to the brim with psychedelic orange tins, useful for when the apocalypse hit.

Turns out, it was nothing that intriguing. The supermarket had a bulk discount deal on tomato soup.

Dad was also on a slippery slope. The other day, I caught him punching the remote control at a blank TV screen, surrounded by dirty, tea-stained cups and chewing on the dregs of last year's Christmas biscuit tin. Worryingly, the TV wasn't even plugged in.

It was bleak.

'Extreme stupidity, more like,' Finn scoffed, interrupting my thoughts.

'Actually, I'm thinking of treating myself to some new threads,' I lied, ignoring him.

'New training gear, maybe,' said Koby encouragingly, tilting his head towards my hoodie, which admittedly had seen better days.

I made a face. 'The parents are bound to notice if I come home with expensive gear, though. You know what my mam's like.'

'A hawk,' Finn said.

'Exactly, notices everything.' Though Mam and Dad were that distracted lately, maybe new clothes in the washing basket wouldn't raise any eyebrows.

'Well, I know exactly what I'm going to do,' Finn said, eyes gleaming as he rubbed the fifty-euro notes through his fingers.

We looked at him.

'Spend. Spend. Spend.'

15

SPECKS CONLON

Emily looked about ready to call it quits. 'Konni-chi-wa.'

Paddy Tarantino grimaced. 'No. No. Konni-chi-wa.'

'That's what I'm saying.'

'Konni-chi-wa.'

'Feck sake, that's what I'm saying, Paddy, you fruit,' said Emily, fuming.

'All right, relax, relax. Let's try it again.'

Paddy nudged me. I held the microphone towards Emily again.

Emily tried again. 'Konni-chi-wa.'

Paddy shook his head.

Emily sighed, deflated. 'Remind me why I am speaking Japanese?'

'Attempting to speak,' I threw in.

'Because my piglets need to become more internationalised. Makes me more money.'

'Makes us more money,' I corrected him light-heartedly. Though, right now, we were making so much money I could barely make sense of it. It gave me goose bumps even to think about it. Finn was the opposite. I could see him doing virtual somersaults every time the word 'profit' was mentioned.

'I didn't even know you gave them voices, Paddy,' I said, thinking back to the piglets.

'Yeah, they can nod their heads, like they're greeting each other,' said Paddy, like a proud parent. 'I'll have them saying "Hello" and a few other words.'

Emily looked up. 'So why exactly am I required?'

'Because I need to throw in a female voice, just to mix things up.'

I grinned. 'Gender equality.'

'Exactly.'

'Paddy, how long more?' We looked up to see a pale, heavily freckled face at the door.

Paddy spun around. 'Specks, we've only just started, mate.'

The freckled face tutted and vanished.

'Who's he?' I said.

'Specks Conlon. His da owns the farm here. But Specks pretty much takes care of everything else.'

'He looks just out of nappies,' Emily said, raising her eyebrows. 'Ten, at the most, I'd say.'

Paddy blinked. 'Close. He's eleven.'

I whistled. 'Cheap labour.'

Paddy fiddled with some buttons on the mixing desk. 'Sly little fox, though. He did me a deal on these recording facilities. Normally charges through the roof.'

'"Facilities". That's pushing it. Considering this is a hay barn, with egg cartons plastered to the wall,' said Emily.

'Sure ya couldn't get a trick by Specks. He's too bloody clever,' said Paddy, waffling. 'Right, Em, go again.'

Emily took a deep breath. 'Konni-chi-wa.'

'Perfect,' said Paddy, clapping. He pressed the button to play it back.

Nothing.

'What the hell!' Paddy punched the button again.

Radio silence.

'Gimme that.' Paddy grabbed the microphone from my hand and tapped the top. Nothing doing.

'Try a reboot,' I suggested.

Paddy unplugged and re-plugged the microphone, unravelled the cable and then tried tapping again. Still nothing. He puffed out his cheeks noisily.

I glanced around. 'Is there another one about?'

Paddy shrugged his shoulders and picked up a walkie-talkie that was lying on the desk. 'Paddy to Base. Paddy to Base.'

Specks's voice came over the line. 'This is Base. Go ahead.'

'The microphone is busted. The microphone is busted. Copy that.'

'Roger that.'

'Is there a spare microphone. Copy that.'

'Roger that. No spare. I'll be over in five. Over.'

Paddy opened his mouth to reply, but the line was already dead.

There was a loud knock on the door.

'Jeez, he's quick,' said Emily wryly.

''Allo, 'allo.' A tanned, scruffy male face appeared around the door. Followed by another. Short and scrawny, both men were struggling with ridiculously oversized backpacks.

'What's up, mate?' said Paddy, glancing up.

'Ah, we are looking for ze campsite.'

Paddy pulled a face. 'Not a clue, sorry.'

'Is there a campsite near here?' I said, turning to Emily.

'Not that I know of.'

They edged further into the room, like crabs. The front man pointed out towards the farm. 'But ze sign says this way.'

They stared at our blank faces for a few moments, then began to retreat backwards out the door.

Suddenly Paddy leapt out of his chair. 'Hold it. Hold it. Where are you guys from?'

'Brazil.'

Paddy's face lit up. 'Brazil. Home of football, eh?' he said, heading an imaginary ball, while also ushering them back into the room.

Paddy shot his hand out. 'I'm Paddy. And you are?'

'I'm Filipe. And this is my brother … eh, Filipe.'

'You're both called Filipe?'

There was lots of enthusiastic nodding.

'Quirky.' Paddy thought for a moment. 'OK, amigos. We'll call you Filipe One. And you back there Filipe Two, yeah?'

Filipe One grinned, showing his whiter-than-white teeth.

I rolled my chair back. There was an unpleasant waft floating my direction. These crusties probably hadn't seen a shower in weeks.

Emily mouthed something at me, playing with the microphone.

'What?' I said, shuffling in.

She mouthed it again.

I leaned in further, lost my balance and toppled straight onto Emily. Her chair tipped over, and we both landed on the floor with a bang, our bodies tangled together. When I looked up, our faces were so close, our noses were practically touching. But, weirdly, neither of us moved. Not straightaway. She locked eyes with me, almost daring me to look away. It seemed to go on for ever. For a split second, the thought to kiss her actually leapt into my head.

She giggled suddenly. 'What I was trying to say was "HIPSTER ALERT",' she boomed, the microphone still in her hand suddenly working again at maximum volume. Her words reverberated around the large barn.

I fell back, startled.

'Oops.' Emily giggled, sinking back onto the floor.

Paddy cleared his throat, keen to get back to his new acquaintances. 'So, you guys speak Brazilian, right?'

'Brazilian Portuguese,' I corrected him, wiping my sweaty palms on my sleeves, as I clambered up from the floor. What the hell had just happened with Emily? I tried licking my lips, but my tongue was matted to the roof of my mouth.

Paddy turned on his charm. 'Filipe, my man, are you and your bro in a rush to wherever it is you're going?'

'Hello, they're homeless, Paddy – remember?' said Emily.

'Would you be able to speak a few words of Portuguese into the microphone?'

Filipe considered this. 'Possibly, amigo.'

'And you?' Paddy said, pointing to Filipe Two.

'He no speak good English. So I talk,' said Filipe One.

Paddy turned to me, rubbing his hands cheerfully. 'Luke, write down all the soccer phrases you can think of. I'm visualising my piglets playing the beautiful game. And if I can promote the video in Brazil first, we'll have a game-changer on our hands, baby.'

Just then, a red-faced Specks appeared at the door. 'Sorry, I got delayed.' He stared at the two backpackers suspiciously. 'Who are you?'

'They're looking for the campsite, apparently,' Emily said.

Specks's face relaxed. 'You got tents?'

Filipe One bowed his head.

'The cost is twenty euro each per night. How many nights?'

The brothers looked at each other, uneasy.

A voice came over the walkie-talkie. 'Young fella, get down here. There's a feckin' heifer loose on the main road.'

'Roger that, Da.'

Specks stared at the backpackers. 'Listen, you can pay me for the one night now, and decide how long you want to stay later,' he said impatiently.

After a lot of shuffling in pockets and in the rucksacks, the brothers finally handed Specks over a mountain of coins.

Specks counted the coins and then nodded. 'The camping field is around to your left, past the playground. No noise after 11 PM. No fires.' He pulled a pad out of his back pocket, scribbled and handed each of them a receipt. 'Tourist information is at reception.'

Emily held her nose. 'Eh, showers, Specks.'

'Ah, yeah, toilet block is out the door on your right.'

'See you in five, guys, for our soccer voice-over session,' Paddy called as they made their way out to find a place to pitch up for the night. 'Didn't realise you were in the camping business now, Specks.'

'Fairly new venture.'

'Going well?'

'Ticking over. Am thinking of doin' up this half of the barn to cater for discos, parties and the like. Da isn't keen, though. So he isn't stumping up the cash.'

Paddy nodded in my direction. 'Well, you know, Luke here might be able to help you out.'

Specks nodded. 'I'd heard rumours.'

'Let's talk afterwards,' I replied. Being honest, I wasn't in the mood to talk loans. But Specks seemed to be at the top of his game. Age eleven. He, of all people, deserved a hearing.

Paddy sat down at the mixing desk. 'Right, let's get back to the Japanese.'

Emily crossed her arms moodily. 'All right, but I'm only doin' this one more time. ROGER that, Paddy.'

$ $ $

'Base to Luke. Base to Luke.'

'Huh?'

Emily touched my arm. 'You all right?'

'Yeah, yeah, just thinkin' about Specks's loan,' I lied, quickening my pace.

'Low risk, what d'you think?'

My mind was racing. A thought occurred to me: I couldn't fancy her, could I? Emily? Finn's cousin? That I'd known since we were in primary school.

Nah. Messy. Pointless anyway, seeing as her and Pablo apparently still had a thing.

I braced myself and turned around to face her. 'Yeah, low risk. He'll get the cash.'

She smiled at me.

I felt my cheeks burn up.

My armpits were dripping sweat.

Disaster.

16
MOSES OBAYA

'Where's he from?

'Station Road.'

'No, idiot. What country?'

'Moses? He's Irish, man.'

'Where are his parents from, then?'

'Town.'

'Jaysus, Gabe. What country did his parents originate from?'

'Africa.'

Finn sucked in a loud breath. 'Africa is a continent, Gabe mate.'

We were outside the shop, waiting for Moses Obaya, who was inside refuelling.

'What's this I hear about gettin' involved with Lochy Mulgrew?' demanded a voice.

We swung around to see Emily, hands on hips.

Finn sprang up and pulled Emily onto the wall. 'Whoa, Em. Sit here. And keep your voice down.'

Emily flicked Finn's hand away. 'Keep your hair on, Finn. Mulgrew is a liability. Just sayin'.'

Finn flashed her a look. 'Lochy is sound. And don't be opening your trap about this to anyone.'

Emily turned to face me. 'Luke, you've a brain. I'm surprised at you agreeing to this.'

I shifted uncomfortably. I still had my doubts about Lochy. Thing was, this shootout could be a game-changer – *if* we managed to bring Obaya into the mix. Speedy vs Obaya. Clash of the titans. Everyone would want a piece of it. It had the potential to blow our other deals out of the water.

'Beat it, Em,' said Finn. 'Look, lads, here's Obaya now.'

Emily studied my face for a moment longer, knowing that she'd hit a nerve.

'Have fun,' she said, jumping down and wandering into the shop.

Finn leapt up and air-punched Obaya's chest. 'Bro, how's the training going?'

Moses Obaya strode past, gulping down a carton of milk. He didn't even blink in Finn's direction. The guy was seriously serious.

Finn attempted to step into Obaya's path, but ended up getting tangled in Obaya's plastic shopping bag. The bag ripped open, and a large container of protein powder rolled down the wet path, stopping at Finn's feet.

Obaya stopped and glared down at Finn. 'What you doing?'

'Obaya, how's the training going these days?' Finn repeated, flustered. He bent down and picked up the container, rubbed it dry with his sleeve and placed it on the wall with a slightly apologetic look.

Slowly, Obaya scrunched the ripped plastic bag in his hand.

Without a word, he shoved the bag down Finn's jumper and punched it into his chest.

I bit my lip.

Obaya frowned, suddenly preoccupied. He sidestepped Finn and strolled off, protein powder under his arm.

'Well, that went well.' I sighed. 'You certainly had him persuaded.'

Finn made a face. 'He's not exactly Mr Chatty.'

'Mo-ses! Mo-ses! Mo-ses Obaya-ya-ya-ya-ya-ya.'

'Hold up,' I said, nodding towards the top of the road. Finn followed my gaze. There was Gabe, shouting and dancing. Then Moses Obaya and Gabe greeted each other as if they were long-lost buds. There was high-fiving. There was air-punching. There was back-slapping. Obaya even cracked a fleeting smile.

'Flippin' hell,' said Finn. 'Who'd have thought it. Gabe's our man. I knew he'd come in handy eventually.'

It turned out Gabe was Obaya's weights partner at the local gym. He was the only one who could keep up with Obaya's frantic bench pressing. Gabe and Obaya were still prancing about, chucking the protein powder to each other, by the time we belted down the street.

Finn clipped the back of Gabe's neck.

Gabe copped. 'Mo, Mo, my mate Finn here has an offer for you. Celebrity shootout. Only the top striker survives.'

Obaya's face straightened instantly. He eyed Finn like a stranger, as if their encounter minutes earlier hadn't happened.

Finn stepped forward. 'Speedy O'Neill claims he is the fastest guy in the school.'

No reaction.

'You anything to say about that?'

I noticed that Finn had stretched right up on his tiptoes. It only brought him as far as Obaya's chest.

Obaya swigged his milk, splashes dribbling down his chin.

He was too cool to rise to that garbage. We were going to have to try a different tack here. Speedy, on the other hand, had been easy to snare. One sniff of a challenge and his eyes lit up like saucers. Or maybe that was the sugar rush, as he'd just consumed three energy drinks and two bananas. No, Obaya wasn't interested in what his competitors thought. He was too arrogant. But his reputation, that was another story.

'People are sayin' that you're losing your pace,' I said.

Obaya sprang up. 'What people?'

I shrugged. 'Dunno. Just heard it down the club house.'

Finn picked it up. 'Saw Joe O'Leary down the pitch yesterday. He puts in the practice sessions, doesn't he?'

I nodded. And waited. O'Leary had started ahead of Obaya in the last two senior matches. And had scored. Both times. As far as I was concerned, O'Leary had got lucky: one deflection and one pathetic goalkeeping error. Still, it should be enough to give Obaya the niggles.

Obaya joined the dots. But he wasn't going to show any weakness. 'This shootout. What's in it for me?'

'Redemption, Obaya mate,' Finn declared. 'The chance to show everybody that you're still number one.'

'Fifty euro?' I offered immediately, recognising the play here. If Obaya wanted to show that he was still top dog, we'd play ball.

'Hundred.'

'Seventy-five.'

Obaya nodded. He scrunched up the milk carton and handed

it to Finn. 'See that bin over there? Sink the carton in the bin and we've got a deal.'

I wondered how Finn would handle this. His aim wasn't the best, if his throw-outs were anything to go by.

'OK, Mo-ses, you're on.'

Finn whispered in Gabe's ear.

Gabe ran over and kicked the bin on either side a couple of times until it loosened from the ground. Gabe heaved it up into his arms and walked towards Finn.

Gently, Finn lobbed the carton into the target.

'That bin's always been wobbly,' said Finn, flashing Obaya a toothy grin.

Obaya's face relaxed.

He was in.

17
THE CASH OUT

'Is it my imagination, or has this shop actually got smellier?' Emily shifted in her chair, surrounded by a sea of five-, ten- and twenty-euro notes littered on the sticky floor. 'And what are these random shoe boxes doing here?' She kicked a box out of her way.

Finn, Koby and I all looked at each other. Mucker McGrath had managed to shift most of his gear, but there was still the odd box floating about.

'Just get on with the job, Em,' said Finn, his eyes roaming greedily over all the money. 'Lads, we've hit the big time here. I'm in heaven.' He scooped up some notes and scattered them up in the air. Gabe joined in, flinging some in the direction of Koby and Pablo, who were sitting on the counter top.

'Guys, stop, I'm nearly done here,' said Emily, her face fully concentrated as she totted up the final figures, shifting bundles of notes around at her feet.

Finn rolled a note up and pretended to smoke it like a cigar.

'Right, the books are balanced,' said Emily, beaming.

'Mr Rafferty would be so proud,' I said.

Immediately, Finn and Gabe stopped messing around.

'Nice one, Em,' said Finn, eyes wide. 'Hit us with it.'

Emily pointed to the bundle on her right. 'So this pile is our liabilities – in other words, the money that needs to stay put to cover future loans.

'And everything over this side is profit,' she said, signalling to the bundle on her left.

I whistled. It was quite a pile, despite all the money bundles that Koby had already shared out.

'Show me,' demanded Finn.

Emily handed her sheets over to Finn, who scanned them. 'Paddy T totally came through for us. We've made a mint on those piggy videos. Easy money, lads, easy money.'

'Strangely, it was the stabbing that did it,' said Koby.

'That deformed pig is a superstar now,' said Finn.

'Not forgetting the Tagged app,' I piped up, looking over his shoulder. 'It comes in a close second.'

'Both of those are our top earners,' said Emily.

'Jo and Lucy added some enhancements,' said Koby. 'That brought in a lot of extra cash.'

'Oh, yeah, the Like and Dislike buttons,' Emily said, nodding. 'You can red- or green-thumb the couples now. It's deadly.'

'Seriously?' I pictured the carnage triggered by people aggressively red-thumbing certain couples.

'It's all confidential. You can't see who is liking or disliking,' Koby said, reading my mind.

Finn tapped the sheet. 'Too right. That app needs to stay outta trouble.'

'You can add a photo to your profile now too,' said Koby.

'Gabe's pic is an absolute cracker.'

'Let me guess. Darth Vader?'

'Not exactly. It's a picture of an Angry Bird lifting a fifty-kilo dumbbell.'

'Caterina has a pic on it. She looks incredible,' Emily said pointedly, pursing her lips. 'Like a supermodel.'

Finn's face tightened. 'Leave it, Em. I don't want to talk about her.'

I raised my eyebrows. Finn and Caterina had obviously hit one of their infamous 'rough patches'.

Finn moaned softly. 'She spends all of her time with that flippin' horse. Pays it more attention than me.'

I made a face. 'I thought you didn't want to talk about it?'

'Horses are mag-nif-i-cent creatures – who wouldn't want to spend time with them?' Pablo said, rolling his shoulders, like he thought Caterina's decision was a no-brainer.

'Yeah, well, Argentinians love their horses, right, Pab?' said Finn. 'I'm sure you spent your childhood riding around bareback in the desert.'

'He's from Buenos Aires,' I said. 'Hardly the outback.'

'What about St Josephs College?' Koby said, veering off topic.

I looked up. 'What about it?'

Koby frowned at Finn. 'You've not told them?'

'I've been distracted,' Finn said, fiddling with his hair. Koby threw me a look. Things with Caterina must really be rocky.

'Spill,' I said.

'Josephs want to join the Tagged app,' said Koby. 'The Sullivans are pushing to go ahead. They have a "contact" in Josephs who is going to supply the student ID numbers.'

I hesitated. 'Is it not a bit risky? Taking it to an outside school?'

'C'mon, Luke, there's only so much money we can make with our school numbers,' Finn said fiercely, quickly forgetting about his girlfriend issues. 'It's the perfect way to expand.'

'The Sullivan sisters have guaranteed that the code will be cast-iron,' Koby said.

Finn put his hand up for a high-five. 'It's another win–win, Lukey.'

I ignored him and went back to Emily's sheet. 'What about the Tubbies? Did they pay everything back?'

'Yeah, yeah. No hassles there.'

'Good job we avoided Fudge Lonergan,' I murmured, making a face. Fudge had been suspended from school having creamed the opposition's goalie in a recent league match.

'What about Koby's new friend on Tagged?' Emily purred.

Koby's eyes widened. 'Was that you?'

Emily swallowed a grin.

Koby pointed at her. 'It was you.'

'What?' said Emily innocently.

'You tagged me with Rosie Byrne.'

Emily burst out laughing. 'Eh, you're welcome. You like her, don't you?'

Koby backed off, looking flustered.

'I don't see her on this list,' I said.

'I have her down as the "Stationery Queen". She's only a few quid behind the Sullivan sisters.'

'Wow. She's taken out ten loans so far and paid them all back.'

Emily shrugged. 'She's totally undercutting the newsagent's in the shopping centre, by the way.'

'What about Mona Lisa Murphy?'

'Annalisa. Pain-ful. Let's see, she finally paid up,' Emily grunted, 'after weeks of chasing.'

I looked down at the notes and breathed in sharply. 'Fifteen weeks late.'

'To be fair, she coughed up all the late fines,' said Koby. 'And we kept multiplying them.'

I pulled out pieces of flattened pizza boxes from between the sheets of paper. 'What's all this junk?'

Emily let out a yelp. 'I think you'll find that on the back of that so-called junk is Gabe's financial accounting. All the names that have opened up savings accounts.'

I turned them over. 'Whoa. Gabe's Batter Burger Deal is flying off the shelves.'

Emily plucked the cardboard from my hand. 'Totally. The hurling team. Football team. Rugby. Basketball. Tennis. He's pretty much sold it to every sports team in the building. Even the girls' hockey team are interested.'

Girls' hockey. No wonder Gabe was looking so lively. We needed a catch-up to double-check the finer details with him. Get up to speed with his sales tactics.

Looking over, I noticed Finn was very quiet and looked pretty miserable. Still brooding over Caterina. 'Let's split this money so,' I said, thinking it might cheer him up.

Everybody fell silent as Emily handed over the various lots of cash.

'Thanks,' I muttered, taking mine and avoiding eye contact. I hadn't seen much of Emily since the awkward incident in Specks Conlon's barn. Probably better that way.

'I want out,' said Koby, almost in a whisper, as he accepted his lot.

'Say what, Kob?' I said, cocking my ear.

'I want out,' Koby repeated, louder this time.

Pablo's face creased. 'Koby, man, are you crazy?'

'You serious?' I said, already knowing the answer. It was written all over his determined little face.

Koby nodded slowly.

'Why?'

'I need the money.'

'For what?'

'A big purchase. Huge.'

Emily elbowed him. 'What's with all the mystery, Kob? Just spit it out.'

'A drone.'

'That's it. A drone,' cried Finn, snapping out of his daze. 'Kob, look around you. We can make enough money for a hundred drones. And this is just the start.'

But Koby's face didn't falter. 'I need the money now, Finn. The model I want has just come down to its lowest price online. So I want to cash out,' he said sternly.

Nobody spoke. Even Emily stopped scribbling.

Finn scratched his head. 'A cash-out deal.'

Koby blinked.

I could see Finn working the calculations in his head. With Koby out of the picture, any cut of the profits would be a lot bigger. For the two of us, anyway.

'So what kind of a deal are we talking, Kob?'

'I just want something fair.'

'So you want to cash out completely? No stake left at all?'

'Yup.'

'You sure? Look at all this dosh.'

Koby shook his head. 'Finn, what's the deal?'

Finn pulled me to one side. 'What you think?'

'Three fifty?' I suggested.

Finn twitched his nose. 'Nah, he'll take three. Let's go with that.'

I sighed. 'Finn, be fair, he did a lot of work with the Sullivans.'

'OK. Three fifty.'

I half-nodded, tuning out. Being honest, I didn't really care that much about the cash out. Let Finn and Koby haggle it out between themselves. It was slowly sinking in that Koby was extracting himself from this project, just when things were hotting up. I glanced down at the bulging notes rolled up in my sweaty hand. I wondered if he could foresee clouds on the horizon.

Koby, naturally enough, accepted the cash-out deal without hesitation. 'Don't worry, I'll still keep an eye on things,' he whispered in my ear, sensing my unease.

'I knew this plan would come good,' said Finn, kissing his money roll as he walked out the door, looking vindicated.

$ $ $

'Come here, Luke. We need to speak to you.'

I skulked into the sitting room, slowly lowering myself onto the arm of the couch, registering that all-too-familiar look on Mam's face, and braced myself for the inevitable.

'Your dad's business … well, it's not doing so good right now.'

'It's closing?'

She nodded slowly. 'We're putting it up for sale. It means that we have to tighten our belts around here. No more luxuries for a while.'

'Luxuries?' I muttered. I tried to recall the last decent thing I'd got. The new woolly hat that Mam had bought me from the second-hand shop hardly counted. Especially an Arsenal one. For me, a Liverpool supporter. I had to pretend to Mam it was grand. Obviously, it was never going near my head.

Mam nodded at the golf clubs that lay strewn across the floor. 'That golf-club membership will have to go, for a start.'

She stared over at Dad, who seemed to have lost his voice completely, and patted his hand. Then she got up abruptly and left the room.

I looked at Dad's strained, unshaven face. I felt a sudden rush of sympathy for him. He looked totally washed out, like the old rag I use to clean my football boots. Worn and crusty. And now, to top it all off, his precious golf was under threat. The only thing that got him out of the house these days.

I fumbled in my pockets. 'Here.'

I thrust the notes that Emily had given me into Dad's hand.

'What this?'

'Put it towards the bills.'

Dad shuffled with the notes. 'There's a lot of money here, Luke.'

'I want to pay my share.'

'Aren't you going to tell me where it came from?'

'I got a job,' I fibbed. 'I told you weeks ago.'

'Where?'

'With Finn's mam. Clearing out some of her vacant properties,' I said quickly, thinking on my feet.

Dad narrowed his eyes, still looking at me.

'You probably weren't listening,' I added in an accusing tone.

'Does your mother know about this?'

'About what?'

'This job.'

'Yeah, yeah.' More lies. But it was unlikely he'd check. He could hardly register the day of the week at the moment.

He held the bundle back out. 'I can't take your money, Luke.'

I lost my patience. 'Just keep it, Dad. Put it towards the broadband so I don't have to spend hours sitting on that toilet, robbing next door's.'

I flicked my head round as I walked out of the room. He'd put the money on the arm of the chair and was back staring at the TV.

But his face seemed slightly more relaxed.

18

JAMES BLAND

'I'll kill him.'

'Calm it, Em.'

'I'll bloody kill him.'

'Jaysus, someone grab her.'

I made a lunge for Emily, catching her waist.

'Let me go.'

Emily jabbed me straight in the ribs, wriggling out from my grasp. Somehow Finn managed to stop her in her tracks.

'What the hell's going on?' I said, panting.

'Emily's having a meltdown.' It was only then I noticed James Burke – or James Bland as we liked to call him – sitting on the wall, spinning a rugby ball in his spade-like hand.

'You think this is a meltdown, Burke. Wait till I get my hands on you,' Emily screeched, still squirming in Finn's grip.

'What have you done to her, Burke?' Finn said, trying to play the protective cousin card. Brave, seeing as James Bland was two years older and at least twice Finn's size. Actually, his thigh was about the width of Finn's waist.

Bland shrugged.

'You liar,' Emily spat. 'You know exactly what this is about.'

'Still hooked on me, Em?' said Bland, smugly.

Emily flared her nostrils.

'Can't blame the girl, really. I'm quite a catch,' said Bland, in his usual monotone voice, fixing his cartoon hair back into place.

'I don't think so. I'd get more intelligent conversation out of that rugby ball.'

I smothered a grin. She had a point. Bland might be the school rugby star, but the stone wall he was sitting on had more personality. I could never understand the attraction. The guy had as much appeal as a day-old bag of chips.

'What's going on, Em?' Finn murmured as Emily stopped for breath. 'I thought you two were history.'

'We are. He's been spreading rumours about me.'

'Not rumours. Fact,' said Bland with a smirk. 'I've the proof here. Wanna take a look?'

Emily swung her leg and sprayed gravel in Bland's direction.

Bland chuckled. 'Maybe we should get back together, Em. I sooo miss this.'

'In your dreams.'

'One hundred and twenty tags. Emily Clarke and James Burke. The perfect couple.'

'I already told you. That was nothing to do with me.' Emily kicked the gravel again, frustrated.

'That's strange. You tagged us as a couple. It came directly from your Tagged account.' Bland held out his phone.

'Show me,' I said, grabbing it and scanning the screen.

I handed the phone back to Bland and stared over at Emily. 'He's right. Over a hundred tags.'

Emily shook her head resolutely. 'Nothing to do with me.'

Finn looked at me. 'But you can't tag yourself, that's one of the rules, right?'

I nodded, confused. Something didn't add up.

Bland got up. 'I'll leave you youngsters to it,' he said, bored. He strolled over and stroked Emily's cheek. 'We had our time, Clarke. Time to face facts, it's over between us. I've moved on.'

She flinched. 'Don't touch me.'

'You're losing it. Like father, like daughter, I guess,' he whispered.

'What did you say?' Finn snarled, loosening his grip on Emily momentarily. She escaped his clutches, dived forward and furiously high-kicked Bland right where it hurts.

'I should have done that ages ago,' she said, watching Bland double over in pain.

She locked eyes with me. I saw a tear roll down her cheek. Next moment, she was gone.

$ $ $

'Cool it, Finn.' My head was wrecked. Finn's pacing was only making it worse. 'OK, so there was a small hole in the software.'

'A small hole. A gigantic crater, more like.'

'Kob's got it sorted. He's been on to the Hunger Twins and they've guaranteed him that it's fixed.'

Finn kept moving, ignoring me. 'Imagine that prat Bland was able to hack into Emily's account. And he's a turnip. The software must have been as open as this bloody door.' He turned and kicked the door hard, slamming it shut.

I knew Finn was laying it on a bit thick, secretly enjoying that this was my deal slowly unravelling. Still, I decided to let him away with it, given Emily's involvement. 'Do you want me to talk to the twins myself? Put the heat on them a little?'

Finn stopped and slumped onto the bench beside me. 'Nah, not before they release the upgrade with this fix. We don't want to put the spooks on them.'

'Honestly, Tagged is so massive, I doubt anyone will care about the bug.'

Finn said nothing, just picked up his boots and started tying up the laces.

I looked up. 'Why did Bland do it? Hack her account, I mean.'

'Payback.'

'For what?'

'Humiliating him. Emily broke up with him. Not the other way around. And nobody breaks up with James Bland.'

'Seems like a lot of effort to go to.' I wondered did Bland still have a thing for Emily and this was his moronic way of trying to get back with her.

'I've never seen her cry before,' Finn said suddenly.

I said nothing.

'Emily. Not once. Even when we were small.' Finn pulled a lace tight. 'Bland totally overstepped the mark today, pulling out that stuff about Emily's dad. The guy ended up in hospital, you know. All his businesses gone bust. Lost everything. Wiped out. Bang. Gone.'

I knew that Finn's uncle had been involved in some dubious property deals that went sour and recently his business had gone under. But I hadn't realised how bad it had all got.

An image of Dad flaked out in the sitting room popped into my head. Dad was a stepping stone away from bankruptcy himself. Could he be heading down the same road as Finn's uncle? I pushed the thought of hospitals out of my mind.

Dropping my head into my hands, I faced the blunt truth. We had to keep the bank profitable. Hard, cold fact: I needed the money to keep the pressure off at home. The little bundles of cash I'd been strategically dropping around the house were a lifeline.

'Will she be all right?' I said eventually, picturing Emily's ghost-like expression.

Finn spat on the ground. 'Only when Bland is crawling around in his own filth.'

19

THE 100M TEASER

Finn groaned loudly, dragging his hands over his eyes, wrenching down his eyelids and squishing up his cheeks. He leaned in close to the laptop screen, tapping the keyboard repeatedly.

'Playing it over and over isn't going to help,' I said finally.

'Seriously, though, I give Gabe one job to do and look what happens.' Finn turned around sharply. 'Where is he anyway?'

Everyone looked at each other. Me. Emily. Pablo.

'That donkey isn't going to show up here now that he knows you're gunning for him,' Emily said.

Finn rolled his eyes and flopped his head down on the desk. 'Simple instructions. Shoot a video. Speedy and Obaya. Sprint drills. One hundred metre race. It couldn't be easier.'

I shrugged. 'Finn, Lochy's book on the penalty shootout is flyin' it, so it's really not that big a deal.'

Finn sat up. 'Yeah, but this video could really get the word out –'

'The word is out.'

'And quadruple our profits.'

'Eh, Finn, feck sake, look around.'

Everyone looked each other up and down. Fresh threads. Designer runners. Latest phones. Watches. Tablets. Headphones. Even I'd given in to temptation and bought some new gear.

I pointed to the king-size, diamond-studded bag on the table and bit my lip. 'I mean, Em, what the hell is that?'

'It's a handy size, yes,' said Pablo.

I laughed. 'Yeah, if you plan on carrying around a bulldog.'

'Don't pick on me,' said Emily, pouting. She grabbed the handbag and hugged it close to her chest. 'It's designer, limited edition, if you must know.'

'C'mon, we've more money than we know what to do with,' I said.

Finn grunted. 'Speak for yourself.'

I gave up.

'Play the video again, Finn,' Emily said calmly. 'Maybe we can salvage something in it.'

Finn pressed down hard on the laptop. After a few moments of complete blackness, some green fuzz. Then the picture came into focus to reveal an extreme close-up of grass stems. In the background, aside from Gabe's persistent heavy breathing, was the sound of a crowd in the distance. Eventually, the camera panned out to the scene unfolding on the football field:

Mr Morgan blows his whistle sharply and stomps up to the white line. 'Right lads. Sprints. Line up here. NOW.' The boys shuffle around, but its all a bit sluggish.

'Morgan goes ape here,' said Finn. 'Watch his face. He's fit to burst.'

'NOOOW,' yells Mr Morgan, his cheeks inflating like a balloon.

'He's like a puffer fish,' said Pablo, filling up his cheeks.

'He's a bloody tyrant,' said Emily. 'I can barely walk after basketball training yesterday.'

'Aw, does diddums want a chair?' jeered Finn. 'Basketball, seriously.'

'Shut up, Finn,' said Emily, flicking his head from behind.

'That Morgan, he is a raging bull,' Pablo said. 'You heard that he asked the canteen to remove the pie from the menu?'

I gasped. 'What?'

Aside from the chips, the chicken-and-ham pie was pretty much Big Peggy's only edible item.

'Too much fat in the … crumble.'

'Pastry,' Emily corrected him.

'Big Peggy told him where to go, I'd say.'

Mr Morgan ran the school sports department with all the determination, discipline and expectation of a professional team coach. All school sports. No exceptions.

'Remember Morgan's trials for the junior badminton team?' I grinned.

Finn snorted. 'Ha, yeah. Legendary.'

'Started out with his notorious fifty–fifty press-up sit-up test and ended with one poor sod in A&E for dizziness and exhaustion,' I continued. 'Hardcore badminton.'

'He's a total adrenaline junkie,' Emily said, pointing at the screen, which had paused on Morgan's beetroot face.

Finn pressed PLAY again:

Cut to Mr Morgan, who takes a long, hard breath.
'Right lads. HARD. HARD. HARD. That's how I
want to see you run. No wimping out on me now.
Everybody in. Everybody focused. Everybody
pounding hard. The guy next to you is not your
friend. He is not your team mate. In this race, he
is your rival. I repeat, he is your rival.'

'Jaysus, you'd swear it was the Premier League,' said Emily.

'Shhh, Em,' snapped Finn. 'At least Speedy lined up next to
Obaya, like I told him. Luke, who were you running next to?'

'Dermo Flanagan.'

'Dodgy Dermo. No wonder you came sixth. He's a snail.'

'You were only one over from Speedy and you came in the
bottom half.'

'Sprinting's not my speciality, though.'

'Finn man, you were too busy fixating with your golden hair,
eh?' Pablo grinned.

'And where are you in the line-up, Pablo mate?'

'I was sick.'

'Ah, a no-show. Not really in a position to comment then,
are you?'

Mr Morgan gets ready to blow the whistle. The
camera centres on his face. Abruptly, it zooms
into a close-up of his nose.
Further.
Further.
Further.
Until the screen fills with just one flaring nostril.

'Ugh. Gross. I see nose hairs.' Emily shuddered, half looking away. 'Why on earth is Gabe zooming in on this?'

'That is the million-dollar question,' said Finn.

Cut to a pink blur.

Finn whined, chomping at his fingernails, exasperated. 'Like, what is he doing here?'

'Maybe he thought you were looking for something more arty,' I said, smiling despite myself. Gabe had probably done his best. He usually did.

After many minutes of extremely jagged camera movements, a clear picture eventually comes into view. A pair of pink football boots. The camera then pans out awkwardly to include a second pair of black and green boots, just behind.

Finn paused the video, sat back and placed his hands on top of his head. 'I don't know if I can sit through this again.'

'Just play it right to the end, man,' said Pablo. Even he was losing his cool.

In the background, the whistle blows. The boots begin to move. Slow at first. Then quicker and quicker. Sloppily, the camera attempts to follow both pairs of boots up the field.

'How is Gabe keeping up?'

'On his bike.'

'Well that explains the bumps.'

'I know, I feel seasick just watching it.'

'So let me get this right. Gabe just films these boots,' said Emily, smothering her giggles. 'He doesn't show any of the sprinter's bodies at all?'

'Well, he was only supposed to get Speedy and Obaya racing,' I replied. 'But, yeah, it looks like he only filmed their boots.'

Emily howled. 'Ah, Gabe, you gotta love him.'

'Which boot wins? Maybe we can use it, no?' Pablo said.

Finn shook his head. 'You haven't seen the end. It gets better. Watch.'

> Still focusing on both pairs of boots, the camera pans out to show the looming white finish line. Then a loud boom. And another. The camera starts to jiggle.
> Boom. Jiggle.
> Boom. Jiggle.
> Boom. Jiggle.
> Boom. Jiggle.

'What's happening?' said Pablo, his head shaking in sync with the footage.

Finn threw up his eyes. 'Hay fever.'

'Huh?'

'Those strange noises – it's Gabe's sneezing. I forgot about his epic hay fever.'

'And the grass was cut that morning,' I remembered.

> Suddenly, an enormous thud.
> A scuffle.

A howl.

The screen turns black and silent.

Finn slammed down on the laptop keys to pause it.

'Is that it?' said Emily.

'Yup,' said Finn.

'So we don't even see the end of the race?' said Emily, rubbing it in.

Finn's face darkened. 'No.'

'What about Gabe?' I said, thinking about that loud cry at the end of the film.

'I've not seen him since,' said Finn. 'He emailed me the vid.'

'Has anyone?' I said, looking around.

No response.

'You've not checked up on him, Finn?' Emily snapped. 'Some friend you are.'

'Yo, yo, besties.'

I turned to see the man himself standing at the door, both hands outstretched in the air. Water streamed down from his bulging, bloodshot eyes. 'Nice to hear you're all so worried about me. Especially you, Em.' He threw his arms around Emily and let out a colossal sneeze.

Emily wiped her face. 'Ugh, get off me, you donkey.'

He staggered forward, like he'd done a couple of rounds in the boxing ring and come out of it the worst.

Finn jumped on it, sniggering. 'Gabe, or is it Rocky Balboa? The state of ye.'

'How's my work of art, Finn boy?' Gabe said, nodding to the screen.

Finn stood up. 'Don't even start –'

'I take it that's a filming injury?' I interrupted, pointing to the bandages loosely wrapped around Gabe's head.

'Yeah. Fell off my bike.'

'Stop the lights. Were you not wearing your helmet?' I said, incredulous.

Gabe grinned gormlessly.

Emily squealed, air-rubbing his bandages. 'Gabe, you're too funny.'

'So let's see, for some weird Gabe-like reason, that motorbike helmet is attached to you like an extra limb most days, but you forget to wear it when you're on an actual bike,' said Finn, scratching his head.

'Embarking on the somewhat perilous trek across the school pitch,' I added dramatically.

Finn laughed. 'Gabe's personal Mount Everest: a field of freshly cut grass. It's been the demise of many a fine man.'

'When's my next shooting commission, Finn boy?' Gabe said, oblivious.

'Stick to the day job, Gabe.'

20

THE STRAWBERRY MILKSHAKE

We watched as Lena Nowak and Eve McMahon tore strips out of each other, limbs flying. A few other girls tried their best to intervene but just ended up being shoved into the ditch.

'Fake tan?'

'Huh?' I stared at the streaky legs.

'On their legs. It's either muck or it's fake tan.'

'Gross.'

'I thought these were friends, no?' Pablo said, raising an eyebrow as Lena grabbed Eve by the ponytail.

'Not today they're not.'

I turned to Finn, who was bound to have the inside story from Cats. 'What's it all about?'

'A milkshake,' Finn said with a grin.

There was a loud shriek. Lena had Eve on the ground.

'A strawberry milkshake.'

'Go on,' I said, intrigued.

Finn shrugged. 'Lena bought Lochy Mulgrew, her so-called boyfriend, a milkshake and drew a little love doodle on the cup, like a heart and stuff. Fast forward a few hours, and Eve has shared a photo of herself on the Internet. And what's she drinking out of? The cup with the doodle.'

I turned to Finn. 'That's it?'

'That's it.'

'Seems a lot of … how you say it? … drama … over a milkshake,' said Pablo finally.

'Bingo, Pablo mate. But that's women for ya,' Finn said all-knowingly. 'Everything's a feckin' big deal.'

I watched as Lena and Eve rolled around the grass. Lena certainly had the upper hand, with all her weight training for basketball. Unless Eve was a secret MMA enthusiast, this was going to be swift and ruthless.

I pondered Finn's story. With Lochy involved, there was bound to be more to it. 'Why would you give someone a used milkshake cup, though?'

'Who knows, Lukey? Maybe poor Eve was dyin' of thirst and desperately needed rehydrating.'

'That's only half the story,' said Koby, who'd just appeared.

The crowds were beginning to grow. I glanced over my shoulder, back at the side entrance of the school. 'We're gonna get sprung here any minute.'

'Tell us the rest so, Kob,' said Finn.

Koby frowned. 'Are you sure you want to know?'

'Spill.'

Koby sighed loudly. 'Apparently Eve "convinced" a load of people to nominate her and Lochy as a couple on Tagged.'

'You're kidding me? Even though Lena and Lochy are goin' out?'

'Yup.'

'And Eve and Lena are friends?'

'Yup.'

'Whoa. Who knew that Eve McMahon was such a viper?' said Finn, almost in admiration. He turned back to watch her, fascinated.

'There's more,' said Koby.

'YOU STUPID COW.'

We all turned back to the action.

Lena was lying on top of Eve, arms restrained. 'You can't get your own fella, so you go and steal MINE.'

'Lochy came chasing me,' Eva gasped.

'LIAR.'

'Just cos you can't hold onto a bloke.'

Out of the corner of my eye I spotted Lochy, watching from behind the wall. He beamed over, giving us two big thumbs-up.

'He looks pretty pleased with himself,' I said.

Koby followed my gaze. 'That's what I was trying to tell you. Lochy has a bet on that he could get two girls to fight over him – like, physically fight.'

'The dirty dog,' said Finn. 'Who was the bet with?'

'TT Doherty.'

Pablo scrunched up his face. 'Who?'

'Alan the Third Doherty. TT Doherty for short,' I replied, grim-faced. 'He's bad news, trust me.'

Finn whistled, deep in thought. 'TT Doherty, bloody hell. Mulgrew is comin' up in the world. He's messin' with the big boys now.'

A loud piercing howl broke up the conversation. 'Whaaat aaare youuu doing?'

'Feck. It's Shiner.'

We turned to see Miss Shine. Small, but deadly. She darted

towards the girls, a hockey stick in each hand. Despite her tiny frame, within seconds she had both girls restrained, pinning their jumpers to the ground like tent pegs. It was hugely entertaining to watch.

$ $ $

I stared into my locker, trying to focus on the books I needed for homework.

Finn sidled up to me. 'I know what you're thinking. Relax, Luke. Seriously, it's not a problem.'

In my mind, I connected the dots. With Lochy doing business with TT Doherty and us connected to Lochy, we were only a banana skin away from being mixed up with TT Doherty ourselves. And TT Doherty was not someone you wanted to play with. Only this year, he nailed four first-years to the wall, just for overtaking him in the corridor. They were found dangling by their jumpers, tears in full flow. And that was tame for TT. Put it this way: they got off lightly.

TT's family were on the dodge side too. The Dohertys had a revolving-door relationship with the local cop shop. There were rumours that TT's da had spent time in prison. And that TT's two older brothers had been questioned by the Special Branch for handling counterfeit goods.

Finn just didn't get the connection. Or didn't want to.

'What are you looking so pleased about?' said Finn suspiciously, watching Emily.

'Nothing. Nothing at all,' said Emily innocently, slamming her locker door shut. 'Just feeling deliriously happy.'

'You and Pablo kiss and make up?'

'Shut it, Finners.'

'Ah-ha. He's still chasing the older women then.'

There were rumours circulating about Pablo and some fifth-year. Unconfirmed. I glanced over at Emily, who was busy ignoring Finn and diligently checking the contents of her schoolbag. She didn't look too bothered.

'What's all this about Lochy Mulgrew and TT Doherty?'

Finn smiled lazily. 'Just a small wager, Em. Nothin' to get in a fizz about. It's all under control.'

Emily gave me the daggers. She'd connected the dots too.

'Your head's getting so big these days, Finn, I'm surprised it fits through the door,' she observed, still looking at me.

Next minute, a loud squeal. 'Holy moly. What are *they*?' Emily was pointing at Finn's feet.

Finn grinned, leg outstretched, showing off a pair of black-and-gold designer trainers, with fake diamonds encrusted along the sides. 'Little beauties, aren't they?'

Emily coughed. 'Ahem, bit much for me.'

'Limited edition.'

I sat up. 'How much did they set you back?'

Finn made a face. 'Not that much.'

'Don't tell me you spent all your split on those?'

'Bling is all in, Lukey.'

'I'll take your word for it.'

21

THE ARTFUL DODGER

Miss Shine tossed the phone on her desk and tapped the screen with her long nail.

'Boys, I've spoken to countless people about this Tagged app. The same names keep coming up.'

She paused and looked each of us straight in the eye. Me. Koby. Pablo. Finn.

'Yours,' she said, pointing at me. 'And yours. And yours. Mr Kowalski, I'm surprised at you. And, of course, no party is complete without you, Mr Fitzpatrick.'

Miss Shine sat down and crossed her arms.

'Explain.'

Nobody budged.

'Mr Morrissey?'

My heart sank. She glared up at me expectantly, not blinking. I stared back. Exchanges with Miss Shine inevitably went this way. A showdown of mental strength. But she never had to wait long for her opponent to break. I could already feel my cheeks flaming.

'Still waiting for an answer, Mr Morrissey.'

I sat rigid. One false move with Miss Shine could be fatal.

Still no blinking. She was a lizard on two legs.

Eventually, feeling the intense pressure, I half-shrugged.

Miss Shine clucked triumphantly. 'I knew it.'

'What's the damage, Miss?' said Finn finally, conceding defeat. He was right. It was futile going up against her. Better to cut our losses, limit the damage and avoid her uncovering anything else.

'The "damage", as you so eloquently put it, Mr Fitzpatrick, well, I'm afraid it's an out-and-out school ban on this Tagged app.'

Finn's body slumped forward. 'Wha –?'

Miss Shine raised her hand to object. 'I don't want to hear it. Count yourselves lucky you're all not up for suspension, or even expulsion, for tampering with the school IT system.'

She had a point. Mind you, technically, it should've been the Hunger Twins on the hook for that. Somehow they had managed to squirm their way out of it by smiling, bouncing their frizzy mops and playing dumb.

'Not to mind girls scrapping like animals in the schoolyard.' She held up a sheet of paper. 'And then to top it off, there's this complaint.'

'What complaint?' said Finn sharply.

Miss Shine lowered her glasses. 'Watch your tone, Mr Fitzpatrick. A complaint from James Burke.'

'Bland,' Finn blurted loudly.

'James Burke,' Miss Shine repeated, staring coldly at Finn.

There was a gentle tap on the door. Emily's face appeared.

'Miss Clarke, delighted you could join us,' said Miss Shine, pointing to a spare chair. 'Now we have the complete set. The famous five, huh.'

Emily lowered herself into the seat beside Pablo.

'Back to James Burke. He claims his profile picture was vandalised.'

She turned the sheet around to reveal a photo of Bland's buff torso – with an overblown rat's head pasted at the top of it.

Finn and I started sniggering. Couldn't help it.

'Boys, this is a serious matter. It could easily be viewed as bullying.'

We straightened our faces as best we could.

I noticed that Emily avoided the photograph, her expression deadpan.

Without warning, Miss Shine dramatically ripped the sheet in two. Then she turned and shredded it meticulously into small pieces.

Behind her back, Finn dived over and clipped Pablo on the knee. Then Emily.

'What?' Pablo mouthed, wide-eyed.

Emily's only reaction was a slight twitch of her eyebrow.

Gradually the penny dropped for me too. Emily. No wonder she'd been floating around in such a good mood. She'd got her revenge on Bland. But she'd had help. There was only one person who could sweet-talk the stony-faced Sullivans into hacking Bland's Tagged account and changing his profile picture. Not Koby. But our local Argentinian girl-magnet.

'I'm also going to throw in a week of detention each.'

As Miss Shine scribbled furiously, beside me Pablo began to hum gently, completely oblivious.

After a moment, Miss Shine looked up.

'Who's that humming?' she snapped.

She narrowed her eyes. 'Mr Silva, is that you?'

Immediately, Pablo turned on the charm. He smiled politely

at her, flashing his brilliant white teeth. 'Yes, yes, I'm so sorry, Mizzz Shine. It just happens. I do not know I'm doing it.'

'Sing, please, Mr Silva.'

'I'm sorry?'

'Sing something for me. Now.'

Pablo turned to me, blind-sided. I shrugged my shoulders. I'd no idea what was going on either.

Miss Shine slammed down her pen. 'Pablo. Please sing a song this instant.'

Pablo's eyes widened. Hesitantly, he started murmuring. After a minute, though, a definite tune began to emerge. It sounded vaguely familiar. Eventually I copped it: Liverpool soccer chant. Odd choice for a Barcelona supporter.

Later he told us that, inspired by Miss Shine's bright red suit, it was the first thing that popped into his head.

'Somewhere in there is a singer, Mr Silva. But we need to be able to hear you. Do you suffer from nerves?'

Pablo raised his eyebrows.

'Are you ner-vous, Mr Silva?'

'No, no, Mizzz Shine.'

'Louder then. Sing louder.'

Pablo started warbling again, turning up the volume this time. To be fair, the sound wasn't glass-shatteringly tragic, despite Emily's mock protests and exaggerated ear-blocking actions beside him.

After a while, Miss Shine threw up her hand to call a halt to it. She tapped her pen on the desk, watching Pablo, who looked increasingly uncomfortable. 'As you know, I'm in charge of the school musical. This year's production is *Oliver*, and opening night is in three weeks. I'm looking for a replacement for the part of the Artful Dodger, as my current Dodger, Maurice Kane, has got chicken pox. And I think I've just found that person.'

'Me?' Pablo gasped, realisation kicking in. He wrinkled up his nose at the thought of it. 'No, no, no, no, Mizzz. A musical. Not cool.'

'That is a pity, Mr Silva. I look quite favourably on anybody who is part of our school-musical family.'

Beside me I could feel Finn shifting in his chair and fidgeting with his sleeves.

'Very favourably.'

'I'm sure Pablo here could be persuaded to join the musical, Miss Shine,' said Finn, seizing his opportunity.

Miss Shine sat back in her chair, swinging gently from side to side, all the while watching Finn like a hawk. 'What have you got in mind, Mr Fitzpatrick?'

'Maybe a bit of breathing space with the app, Miss,' Finn said boldly.

Miss Shine raised her eyebrows. 'I tell you what, Mr Fitzpatrick. You give me an all-singing, all-dancing Pablo Silva, and I'll put your phone app up in front of the school council. Let them decide its fate.'

Finn made a face.

'That's my one and only offer, Mr Fitzpatrick,' said Miss Shine coolly.

Finn nodded, ignoring the warning shots coming from Pablo's direction.

'Great. Mr Silva, I look forward to seeing you at rehearsals,' said Miss Shine, standing up. 'Don't worry, I'm not expecting any record-label giants to be beating down the door.'

'How're you gonna persuade Pablo to do this musical?' I said under my breath as soon as we'd all been shuffled out of the office.

'Simples,' Finn said. 'We'll pay him.'

'What about the Tagged app and the school council?' I wondered.

'I'm happy to take my chances with the school council. Who knows, they could be open to some persuasion.' He nabbed the back of Emily's jumper. 'Not so fast, Em. We need to talk about that hack job you did on Bland's picture.'

Emily froze. 'To congratulate me, I hope?' she said, voice cracked.

Finn's mouth opened, but I caught his arm.

Slowly, Emily turned and looked at us, her face still raw with anger. 'Don't tell me, you're having a little cry because your stupid app is on the hook. Boo flippin' hoo.'

'Pretty high price for revenge, Em.'

Emily's temper flared. 'Don't go there, Finn. I'm warning you. Just do not go there.'

For once, Finn kept his trap shut.

22

ALAN THE THIRD DOHERTY

Finn stood on his tiptoes. He tapped the shoulder of the lad in front of him. 'What's the queue for?'

'To sign Obaya's cast.'

'Huh?'

'The cast. For his leg.'

Finn's breathing quickened. 'His what?'

'Haven't you heard?'

But Finn had already sprinted up the corridor towards the canteen, winding between the crowd. I legged it after him.

'Obaya, what the hell?'

Obaya was sitting in front of a massive bowl of pasta. His right leg, propped up on a chair, was completely encased in a bright white cast, one half already covered in scribbles. Finn pushed past the gang who were clamouring to sign it.

Obaya glanced up briefly from hoovering his spaghetti and half-nodded impassively at Finn.

Finn wiped the beads of perspiration from his forehead. 'What, what happened?'

'Touch rugby.'

I frowned. 'But you don't play rugby.'

'Just messin' about.'

'H– how?'

Obaya put down his fork. 'I was makin' for the try line, when, bang, tackled to the ground. Fell badly. Twisted the leg.'

I winced. 'How long are you out?'

'Ten weeks. Maybe more.'

That put Obaya out for the rest of the season. The hole in the senior soccer team would be massive. 'Man, that's rough.'

'Aren't you left-footed, though?' Finn said. 'Maybe you –'

'Finn, seriously, the guy is on crutches,' I said. There was no way Obaya could do the shootout. Plus he looked pretty devastated.

Finn backed off.

'That'll teach you to try rugby,' I said, smiling sadly at Obaya. 'Take it easy, man.'

Obaya's eyes opened wide. 'Don't worry, next time I'll get my tackle in first. Burke won't know what hit him.'

Finn stopped. 'Wait – Burke. Do you mean James Burke?'

'Got it in one,' Obaya said without looking up.

Finn's face tightened.

He dragged me away from the table. 'I don't believe it. James Bland. Again.'

'We don't know that he did it on purpose.'

'Cop on, Luke. This is no coincidence. Bland knew damn well that we had Obaya lined up for the shootout.'

I thought Finn was overestimating Bland. He wasn't that intelligent. 'But Bland could hardly have planned this.'

Finn's eyes narrowed. 'No, he saw his opportunity and took it. He was out for revenge for that profile-picture play. Sure he was totally humiliated.'

I gazed over at Obaya, whose remaining season lay in tatters. I couldn't ignore the growing feeling of unease in the pit of my stomach. This thing was growing legs and beginning to get beyond our control.

'This is our fault, Finn. We got Obaya mixed up in all this.'

Finn put out his hands in protest. 'Hold up, Luke. We didn't tell Bland to tackle Obaya to the ground. He did that all by himself.'

'Greetings.' We looked up to see the large shadow of TT Doherty looming over us.

'TT,' said Finn warily.

He reached out and put an arm around each of our shoulders. 'There they are, my new business partners.'

I pulled away. He grabbed Finn in a head lock, tossing his hair. 'Didn't Lochy tell you guys?'

'Tell us what?' I said, my breath quickening.

Roughly, TT released Finn, who stumbled forwards. 'He's transferred ownership of his betting business to me. So it looks like we'll be doin' business together from here on.'

'You ... own the b-b-betting b-book?' I said, desperately trying to process the enormity of this development.

TT cracked his knuckles. 'You see, Lochy owed me some winnings and he failed to pay out. So he suggested I take the book instead of payment.'

I'd not seen Lochy about for days. No wonder he had vanished.

'Wait. Lochy owes us money too, though! For his loans,' said Finn, finding his voice.

I stared at Finn, who was matting his hair down. We could surely kiss goodbye to any repayments from Lochy now that he'd given away his book.

'I heard about your little banking venture. So adorable. Not my problem, though. That's between you and him.'

'But what about the penalty shootout? We had a percentage deal with Lochy on the profits from all bets placed.'

'Yeah, that was a pretty sweet deal. But I'm afraid those agreements don't transfer.'

'But Lochy and I signed a contract.'

TT wobbled his bottom lip. 'Shame.'

'It was in the terms and conditions.'

TT grabbed Finn's arm. 'I make the terms and conditions now, my friend.'

Finn's mouth snapped shut.

TT's face relaxed. 'So what's your next move?'

We both stared at him, white faced.

TT leaned against the wall, popping his knuckles again. 'That shootout needs to go ahead, lads. Otherwise you'll have a lot of void bet refunds to hand back to punters.'

'Hold on. Why would we refund the bets?' The words had slipped out of my mouth before I could stop them.

'New rules,' TT said, snarling. 'So you'd better do the job. Or I won't be happy. And who d'you think I'll take my unhappiness out on?'

We shuffled back.

TT took another step towards us, his face threateningly close. He grabbed our chins, one in each hand, and wiggled them up and down, like we were nodding puppets. 'TT, you handsome devil, we will find a replacement for Obaya as soon as possible.'

I turned away, as his breath stank.

TT let go. 'Great, that's settled then. Nice doin' business with you bucks.'

He gave us a thumbs-up as he walked away.

23

BATTER BUCKET

I skidded out the side gate, trying to ignore the loud rumbles from my stomach. Double maths last thing on a Monday was the worst. I collided with Finn, who was cowering at the wall.

I stumbled backwards. 'Whoa, Finn. Watch it.'

'Luke.' Finn leaned over, breathless. 'Luke, small problemo.'

I stopped, taking in Finn's unusually dishevelled appearance. 'Fresh cut?' I grinned, raising my eyebrows at the fuzzy hair tufts sprouting from his head.

Finn frowned at his reflection in his phone screen. 'Just got leap-frogged by Mona Lisa Murphy.'

I smothered a laugh. 'What?'

'She caught me by surprise, all right. Wrestled me to the ground. I just about got away from her.' Finn rolled up his sleeve and examined his arm. 'I swear she dug those witch nails into my arm. Yeah, look, permanent scar, that.'

I leaned in to examine the result of the alleged assault, but could barely see the hint of a mark, let alone any lifelong damage. Still, this was very un-Mona-Lisa-Murphy-like behaviour. She was mouthy, but she didn't have a tendency towards physical violence. 'Savage. What the hell's got into her?'

But Finn didn't reply, distracted by a commotion at the school entrance. He scrambled at the wall and peered over. 'Bloody hell. Here she is.'

I stood up on my tiptoes. Mona Lisa was at the main entrance, barging through the crowd, yelling and throwing shapes. She did a quick U-turn and pounded towards us.

'Uh-oh.' Quickly, Finn crouched down behind my back. 'Don't move, Luke.'

Mona Lisa appeared at the gate, hands on hips, sucking in her cheeks. 'You seen Finn Fitzpatrick? I know for a fact that he came out this way.'

I shrugged my shoulders casually, body paralysed to the spot. 'Nah, didn't see him.'

Mona Lisa edged out, gazing up and down the road.

I shuffled, robot-like, trying to conceal Finn from her view.

Suddenly, Finn grabbed hold of my leg and sneezed loudly.

Mona Lisa's face twisted, immediately suspicious. She stepped forward, looking dangerous.

Behind me, I could hear the sound of muffled laughter.

Bloody Finn.

To deter her, I did the only thing I could think of: kick-started a sneezing fit. I sneezed, softly at first, building it up to loud bursts, intermixed with sporadic fits of the giggles.

Mona Lisa looked me up and down, like I was a clown. 'What's wrong with you?'

'Nothin',' I managed, eyes watering and stomach muscles contracting.

Overcome with the effort of trying not to laugh, I lost my balance and toppled back, my bum cheeks whacking Finn straight in the face.

'Nice,' Finn hissed, punching me.

I bit down hard on my lip and breathed in slowly, trying to regain control. 'Look, Murphy, I've gotta head. I've not seen Finn today. What d'you want him for anyway?'

'Gabe O'Rourke sold me a savings deal. And according to him, Finn Fitzpatrick is the mastermind of this bank tragedy.' Mona Lisa jabbed her finger in the air aggressively, like she was picturing Finn's face. 'You give Finn a message from me: tell him that I want the deal I was promised or things spiral. End of.'

She stomped off back towards the school.

I exhaled loudly. 'What the hell was all that about?'

Finn leapt up, stretching out his legs. 'She's lookin' to close her savings account. Not overly impressed.'

'No, really? But she's a ray of sunshine,' I said, rolling my eyes at the understatement.

'Claims she didn't get the deal she was promised from Gabe.'

We heard a faint rustle at the gate.

Finn dragged at my jumper. 'C'mon. Before she turns up for round two.'

We pegged it down the road.

Eventually, I caught my breath. 'So what exactly was Mona Lisa promised?'

It suddenly occurred to me that we'd never bothered nailing Gabe on the finer points of his savings plan. Rookie mistake.

Finn gritted his teeth. 'Apparently, when Gabe negotiated the deal with the lads down the chippy, he was actually eating a Batter Bucket. And not the Batter Burger Meal Deal. The feckin' hog.'

I wondered where this was leading. 'Bucket – a Batter Bucket?'

'Y'know, one of those jumbo yokes, where everythin' in it is covered in batter: battered burgers, battered sausages, nuggets –'

'Sounds like our Gabe's on a health kick,' I said.

'Onion rings, pizza and mountains of chips,' Finn continued.

I stuck out my tongue. 'Battered pizza, really?'

'Sounds totally off, but trust me, it's genius. Try it, my friend.'

'Wait, what's all this got to do with Gabe's savings deal?' I said.

Finn's face dropped. 'Well, the Batter Bucket usually feeds four to six people.'

I shrugged. I still didn't get it. 'So Gabe's a Cookie Monster. Old news.'

'No, No. Luke, think. The bucket costs twenty euro,' Finn spat out, raising his voice slightly.

He nodded at me vigorously.

Suddenly I had an image of Gabe, happily gorging on his Batter Bucket, in a glorious post-training haze of grease, sweat and vinegar, and nodding away gormlessly to whatever guff was thrown his way by the lads down the chippy. Like the outrageous suggestion to hand over the price of a Batter Bucket each time any of the lads agreed to save a wad of money with the bank.

My stomach churned. 'Damn, so Gabe's deal was to pay a twenty-euro bonus for every deposit saved?' I winced, praying I wasn't right.

'Finally, he gets it,' cried Finn, throwing his hands up. 'Yeah, every time someone saves over fifty quid, they get the Batter Bucket bonus. A twenty spot.'

'Jaysus, that's almost a fifty per cent bonus,' I muttered to myself. No wonder people were queuing around the block to sign up to Gabe's savings scheme. It was a gold rush.

I gritted my teeth. We should never have let Gabe out of our sight. This had the potential to snowball into payouts in the hundreds when people started closing their accounts. It would clean us out.

'Face it, Finn, this is a whopper. Do we have any idea how many signed up altogether? And how much money people have saved so far? And Mona Lisa Murphy, I mean, c'mon, she'll never keep it zipped. Everyone knows she has a gob the size of a bowling ball.'

Finn caught my sleeve. 'Listen, keep cool, Luke, not a word to anyone. I'll fob Mona Lisa off with a story.'

'Ha! Right, so just sit tight and wait for the angry mob to show up?'

Finn puffed his cheeks. 'No, no, just need to buy us some time. Keep that money tap flowing.'

I shook my head impatiently. Finn was too blinded by the cash to see the wrecking ball swinging our direction. 'Finn, we need to grab hold of this now, 'fess up and offer all our savers a sweetener to keep them happy.'

I caught my breath.

'Or give everyone their money back. Say the savings thing was a mistake,' I said, despite knowing this would send Finn into a tailspin. 'Blame Gabe and his idiotic bucket meltdown.'

Finn's face dropped, horrified. 'What? Refunds? No. That's a tad extreme.'

'Think about it, Finn. We'll have a riot on our hands if everyone finds out they're not getting the deal that Gabe promised. And remember, we're talkin' about all the sports junkies in the building. They'd annihilate us.'

I pictured an army of six-pack abs marching towards us.

'Plus anyone else Gabe's sold this lemon to,' I added.

Finn waved his arm. 'Listen, I'll take care of Mona Lisa.'

'Let me guess. You'll pay her off?'

Finn smirked. 'You know me so well.'

I shook my head. Finn was way off target this time. Mona Lisa was no pushover. 'Not gonna work with her. Underneath all that frizz, Mona Lisa's a viper.'

'Leave her to me. I'll get us a few weeks' breathing space. Then we come clean to everyone and offer the sweetener.'

I thought quickly. Finn was right about one thing: we needed to keep the cash coming in. Especially with TT Doherty lurking around.

'All right, hopefully we can keep a lid on it until then,' I said doubtfully, an image of Mona Lisa and her bowling-ball gob floating into my mind again.

'Good man.'

I slowed the pace as we reached the corner of my road and pulled my old trainers out of my bag.

Finn jostled one from my hand. 'Whoa, old school. I thought you'd chucked these wheels?'

I reefed it back. 'Not yet.'

Finn prodded his finger at the front of the trainer. 'What're all those weird orangey zigzags?'

'You don't wanna know.' I groaned, stifling a laugh. 'Remember that massive rip? Mam tried to sew it. Good as new.'

Finn shuddered. 'Jaysus. Bin them quick, bro.'

I stuffed my new trainers into the bottom of my bag. 'I can't prance around in these newbies at home. Mam would spot them a mile off and start grilling.'

Strictly speaking, that wasn't the whole truth. I didn't want Mam to feel guilty about a pair of shoes. Things were bad enough at home.

Finn stared at my feet. 'So you swop trainers every day?'

'Trust me, it's not worth the hassle.'

'So long as they are not for public viewing, Lukey. House shoes only.'

'And I was gonna wear 'em into town tomorrow,' I said, poker-faced.

Finn looked alarmed. 'Seriously? If the lads from town spotted those bad boys, we'd be laughed out of it.'

I legged it up the driveway.

'What about Gabe?' I called back, even though I already knew the answer.

Finn's jaw hardened. 'New on the menu: one Gabe, deep fried in a crispy batter.'

$ $ $

Later that evening, I got a text from Pablo:

Hey, man, just put twenty fingers on speedboats.

I waited. It usually didn't take Pablo long to correct his predictive-text mishaps. Seconds later, another text:

Sorry, man. Just put twenty euros on Speedy.

As I reread the message, a worrying thought struck me. It appeared TT Doherty was still taking bets for the shootout, even though we'd no opponent for Speedy lined up. My phone buzzed again. This time, a message from Emily:

Newsflash! TT Doherty has topped 200 bets for shootout.

You better find Obaya sub or you could be on the hook for hundreds :-o

Two hundred bets and counting. Meaning we'd be stung for an Olympic-sized swimming pool of refunds if the shootout was a fail.

Straightaway, I dialled Finn's number.

24

THE LOBBYIST

I worked my hand into my jeans pocket, struggling to retrieve the coins that were wedged deep in the corner. Tight jeans were a bad decision. Actually, shorts would've been a better call, even though summer was still months away.

'So, eh, what do you want? It's on me,' I called out awkwardly, raising my hand to block out the surprising heat of the sun.

Katy Doyle beamed at me. 'Ninety-nine, thanks.'

By the time I'd queued, ordered and paid for two ninety-nines in the shop, Katy had gone back outside and was sitting on the wall.

I handed her the dripping cone. Another beaming smile. I knew I shouldn't have let Finn talk me into this. My mind wandered back to the stand-off.

'Listen, Luke,' he'd said. 'It makes perfect sense. Katy Doyle is kingpin on the school council. And we all know that Katy Doyle has a crush on you of gigantic proportions.'

I shook my head. Total denial.

Finn burst out laughing. 'She gives you the goggle eyes every time, mate. Every single time. Back me up here, Em.'

Emily had smiled reluctantly. 'Epic, epic crush, the poor girl.'

'She's cute,' Finn had sung, ignoring Emily.

I shook my head again. 'I won't do it, Finn. No way.'

'Just meet up with her once. Nothing heavy. Bring up the app and see if she'll bite.'

I sighed. 'I feel bad, Finn. Like I'm leading her on.'

Finn slapped me on the back good-humouredly. 'You're overthinkin' it, mate. Even if Katy realises what your agenda is, she'll be sour, but it'll blow over. She'll have forgotten all about it in a few days.'

Emily snorted loudly. 'Katy Doyle is no fool. In fact, she's totally clued in and you're talkin' about her as if she has nothing up here.' She tapped the side of her head. 'And, hello, bribing the school council. A new low, even for you, Finn. This'll end in tears. Guaranteed. Hot, fat tears.'

'C'mon Luke, we really, really have to get this app back on track,' said Finn impatiently, ignoring Emily's rant. 'The Sullivans are about to release a new version.'

'Not this way.'

Finn's face darkened. 'Especially with Gabe's burger blitz teetering on a cliff edge. And TT Doherty in the mix now.'

Finn back-kicked the wheel of his bicycle, sending it hurtling across the road, near to where Emily sat on the kerb.

She sprang up. 'Finn, that could've hit me, idiot.'

I reached for the bike. 'Jaysus, Finn, will ya relax.'

Finn paced up and down, steadying his breathing. 'Surely you really need the cash for –' He stopped.

'For?' I said, meeting his deadpan stare.

Finn hesitated. 'Well, just with things the way they are with your dad's business, I'm sure your parents would appreciate –'

'What, Finn? What would they appreciate?'

Finn shrugged. 'Just with the business closing. And I heard your dad had to sell his van.'

Instantly, something inside me snapped.

I grabbed Finn, drove him forward and pinned him hard against the wall. 'Don't try to play me, Finn. Or talk about my dad or his business.'

In the distance, I could vaguely hear Emily shouting at me to stop. Then I could feel her beside me, her hands trying to prise us apart.

'Get off, Emily,' I said, pushing her away. 'This is between me and Finn.'

I held my body against Finn's with all my strength, clenching my jaw. He tried to scramble away, but my grip was solid.

We locked eyes.

'Luke, that bloody hurts.'

'You knew, didn't you?'

No reply.

'Didn't you?'

'Knew what?' Finn gasped.

'That Dad's business was in trouble. Back when you asked me to join the bank.'

'No.'

I drove him harder against the wall.

'All right, I might've heard something.'

I loosened my grip very slightly.

'From where?'

'I overheard Mam sayin' it.'

I shut my eyes briefly, relieved. At least people at school weren't gossiping about it.

'Look, I should've told you, mate,' said Finn, sounding genuine for once. 'Sorry.'

Finally, I let him go, both of us collapsing to the ground.

I thought of Dad, stuck in a black void, formally known as the sitting room. Of Mam, working night shifts to make ends meet. Of me, perched on the upstairs toilet for hours, attempting to connect to the online world. Of TT Doherty and his foul stench in my face.

Eventually, I got my breath back. 'Katy Doyle. OK, I'll do it.'

Fast forward a few days: I was skulking in the village with Katy Doyle, slobbering on ninety-nines.

'So, how's maths going with Raffo?' I said, breaking the radio silence.

Dumb question.

'Grand,' Katy said politely. 'Hopefully I'll get into the honours class next year. Rafferty is a good teacher. Will you stick with the honours?'

I thought of my mid-term test results. 'Doubt it.'

Cue awkward silence.

'And how's the basketball going?' Another zinger. Get to the point, Luke.

Katy crunched up her nose. 'Hockey, you mean? I play hockey, not basketball.'

'Oh, yeah, hockey, sorry.' Feck sake.

I turned to face her. I noticed ice-cream dribbling down her chin.

'Eh, you've got –' I pointed to her chin.

She wiped it with a tissue, blushing.

I shifted a little further away on the wall. This was getting more awkward by the second.

'So you're on the school council, right?'

Katy nodded eagerly.

'How's that?'

'All right.'

'I'd say it's a lot of work, is it?' I said, almost boring myself at this point.

'Yeah, it's a bit of a pain sometimes, all the meetings and that,' said Katy, wiping some ice-cream drops from her T-shirt. 'Why? You're not thinking of running next year, are you?'

'No way. Definitely not.'

I stuffed the rest of the cone in my mouth and chewed for a minute.

'So, that Tagged app –' I let the words hang in the air. 'You know it, right?'

'Tagged? Oh, yeah, who doesn't?'

I tried to think of my next line.

'Everybody is on it. Pity that it'll get shot down,' Katy said.

I nodded. Then I thought for a moment. 'Hold on, what d'you mean shot down?'

'It won't pass at the school-council meeting, if that's what you're on about,' said Katy matter-of-factly. 'I feel a bit sorry for the Sullivan sisters – they put so much work into it.'

'Why are you so sure that it won't pass?'

'Because of that profile-picture complaint.'

'Right.' Bloody James Bland.

Katy threw me a curious look. 'What's it to you?'

'Nothing really. It's such a deadly app,' I said, waffling. 'And the Hunger Twins put in –'

'Who?'

'I mean, the Sullivan sisters, they put in so much work. Koby, my mate, helped them out with the code and the security.'

'Yeah, well, I think it's a done deal now. After that complaint, it'd be a miracle if it got through council.'

I perked up. 'So there's a chance?'

She threw me a curious look.

'You said it'd be a miracle. There's a chance then?' I said cautiously, anxious not to show my cards too soon.

'Yeah, a teeny tiny one,' she said.

'Is there anyone on the council who'd vote for it?'

'Doubt it.'

I kicked the gravel with my shoe. 'Is there anyone who could be persuaded to vote for it?'

Katy's face tightened. 'Wait a sec. Are you talkin' about … like … bribery?'

'No, no,' I lied. I could hear the strain in my voice. I'd overplayed it.

She stared straight at me, her eyes widening like pools. 'You are.'

I said nothing. Sometimes it's best.

'You wanted to persuade me to vote for the app at the council meeting,' she said, twigging. 'And see who else on the council I could influence.'

She stood up, dismayed.

'Look, Katy, I'm real sorry. I was just helpin' out a mate,' I mumbled, feeling my face heating up like a tomato.

I slumped against the wall as she marched off.

'Ha, got you.'

I glanced up, frowning.

She'd spun back around and was smiling at me, all teeth.

'Relax, Luke. I'm messing around. It's a joke.'

I stared at her, my head scrambled. 'Feck sake.'

Katy bit her lip. 'Sorry, I couldn't resist. You looked so awkward. I'm surprised Finn Fitzpatrick isn't sitting there instead of you. Isn't bribery and corruption more his type of thing?'

I nodded. She hadn't copped that I was specially selected because of the alleged crush. At least that was something.

She sat back down beside me. 'So what's in it for me? If I help you?'

'Money?' I offered in a low voice, recovering quickly.

'That's a start, I guess,' she said carefully. 'I'll need something bigger to convince a majority to vote in favour of the app.'

'Like what?' I asked, suddenly wary.

'The annual school disco.'

'What about it?'

'We've no place to hold it. It's the school council's responsibility to organise it. Two venues have cancelled on us already. I think they're afraid that the TV crew will show up.' She turned to me. 'Find me a venue. And I'll get you the vote.'

'Sweet,' I said quickly, thoroughly relieved.

$ $ $

'I knew it. I knew Katy Doyle isn't as innocent as she looks.'

'Yeah, whatever,' I said, leaning over and running my hands through my hair. My head felt heavy. My touch had been a disaster at training. I'd missed a couple of sitters at the right post.

Finn puffed out his cheeks. 'You're too honest, Luke. That's your problem. Katy saw straight through you.'

I loosened the laces on my boots, saying nothing.

'So what about this disco venue? I presume you were thinkin'
of Specks Conlon's barn?'

I nodded.

'Nice one.'

I threw on a jumper.

'The council vote is next week. So we need to get the cash to
Katy as soon as,' Finn said. Then he sat back, rubbing his hands.
'Back on track. I told you this was just a blip, a temporary blip.'

I stood up, grabbing my bag.

'See, everybody has their price, Lukey boy.'

I stopped and looked back over my shoulder at him. There
was an arrogance to Finn's voice that I just didn't appreciate.

25

THE RINGER

'All righ', bud.'

'Luke, meet my cousin, Clint Mooney. Up from the big smoke.'

'Clint.' I nodded carefully, wondering what this was all about.

Clint immediately dug his boots into the ground, unimpressed. 'Jaysus, the pitch. It's brutal.' His foot sank into a pool of sticky slop, almost toppling him over. 'It's a bleedin' death trap, Fitzy.'

I raised my eyebrows at Finn.

Finn hopped from one foot to the other. 'Ta-da! Meet our super sub. Obaya's replacement for the shootout.'

I stared from Clint to Finn to Clint, who was now stomping around the goal area, examining it closely and cursing repeatedly.

'I've never heard you mention this cousin Clint before,' I said eventually.

'Yeah, he's like a second cousin.' Finn waved dismissively. 'But he's got a killer left foot, Lukey. Killer.'

'Right, so you think TT Doherty's gonna agree to swop him in for Obaya, just like that.'

Finn made a face. 'There's nothin' in Lochy's book about

changing the players at the last minute. I checked the small print.'

I found that hard to believe. But then Lochy was notorious for his hidden loopholes to avoid payouts.

'We can't just rock up with a total stranger, Finn. He doesn't even go to school here. I mean, how're we gonna persuade people to bet on him? A total unknown.'

Finn's phone beeped. He smiled triumphantly. 'Sorted, Lukey. Take a look at this.'

I glanced at the screen. 'You hacked into Clint's account?'

'Nah, nah, it was easier than that. I started a few rumours about Clint Mooney and his "extraordinary" talents – shared a few fake posts about him, that he'd gone for trials at Spurs, now Everton are interested – and, bingo, all the online sheep fell for the bait.'

'What am I looking at?'

'Here, see, soon everybody will be sharing it online. Clint Mooney vs Speedy O'Neill. Penalty shootout of the decade. It's gonna be huge. I'd better warn Speedy that it's all about to kick off.'

'Whoa, we've not agreed on Clint yet.' I watched as Clint head-butted a goalpost. 'Isn't he a bit of a loose cannon?'

'Clint knows the score, Luke. He'll be on his best behaviour.'

Whatever that was.

I crossed my arms. 'So how are you related exactly? You and Clint?'

Finn exhaled dramatically. 'All right, all right, you win. So he's not technically my cousin.'

'Huh. Who is he then?'

'Let's just say he's a friend of the family.'

I shook my head. Maybe I was better off not knowing.

I wondered what exactly was in it for Clint. 'So what's this gonna cost us?'

Finn's face lit up. 'That's the beauty of it. Not a bean.'

'Nothing at all?' I said doubtfully.

'Well, not exactly nothing. Just an opportunity.'

'What do you mean, opportunity?'

'Clint fancies himself as a bit of a rapper. Has ambitions to break into the music industry.'

As if on cue, Clint let rip and tried to scale the fence, sliding back down with a bump.

'Er, Clint mate, where you off to?' Finn shouted.

Clint cracked his knuckles loudly. 'Ah, nowhere, bud, nowhere. Just a little technique I picked up to help me relax when I feel on edge, y'know? The state of your pitch is botherin' me, big time.'

Finn whipped out his phone and started videoing Clint's frantic commando-style efforts up the fence.

'Anyway, Clint's got big plans to make a music video for his latest rap. And he's aware of my close relationship with Paddy T, videographer extraordinaire,' he continued.

'Have you run this by Paddy?' I couldn't see Paddy Tarantino working with this wildcard. By now, Clint had monkey-climbed the fence and was perched at the top, waving over to us triumphantly.

Then again, Paddy T did work with animals most of the time.

'Clint will be thanking me in his acceptance speech when he wins his first Grammy. I can see it now: Clint Mooney, the new gangsta of rap. The rest, as they say, will be history,' said Finn, ignoring my question.

I watched as Clint used the fence as a punchbag. No way was I convinced that Clint was our man. 'Finn, I'm not so sure.'

'Luke, we've no choice. Think about it. Who else can we get to step up against Speedy at this stage? And if this shootout doesn't happen and we get nailed with the bet refunds ...'

He didn't finish the sentence. He didn't need to. The bet refunds would wipe us out. It'd be the deathblow for the bank.

'Does it ever stop rainin' here, bud?' Clint reappeared, pulling his hood up as light drops began to fall. 'Pourin' outta the heavens, it was, earlier. Makes the pitch lethal to play on. In ribbons, it is. No bleedin' clue how yis do anythin' on it.'

'Slidin' tackles all round,' I quipped, but Clint seemed completely preoccupied with the sub-standard facilities.

Finn caught Clint by the sleeve. 'Clint, call me "cuz". Makes it more legit.'

Clint slapped Finn hard on the back. 'The rain's no good for me hair either, cuz. Makes the gel all sticky, like.'

Carefully, Finn reshaped his own hair. 'Just style it out, cuz.'

I breathed out, filling my cheeks. It was going to be a long week.

$ $ $

Gently, I placed my spoon on the kitchen table, trying to ignore the bile rising from my stomach. I glanced over at Dad, who was staring into the steaming orange abyss, eyes watering.

'You not eating?' said Mam, quick as lightning.

'I forgot, I need a tenner tomorrow for school, a science trip,' I said, hoping to veer the subject away from the tomato soup.

Judging by the dog-tired expression on Dad's face, he probably felt the same.

'Strange,' Mam muttered.

I turned around. Mam was leaning against the kitchen counter, frowning into her purse. She pulled out a bundle of notes. 'I'm sure these weren't here yesterday.'

Quickly, she flung them on the counter, like they were burning her fingers. 'These weren't in my purse yesterday. I know it.'

Dad grunted. 'Just give Luke the tenner.'

Mam scratched the side of her head. 'Money just keeps appearing. Like the notes I found in my jeans pocket the other day.'

I sat back. I'd been strategically placing little money bundles around the place lately. Maybe slipping notes straight into her wallet was a step too far.

I hopped up. 'Old age, Mam. Face it, your brain is turning to mush.'

I whipped a tenner from the counter, accidentally knocking over her handbag in the process and spilling the contents all over the floor.

Mam dived down. 'Leave it.'

I spotted an electricity bill, with 'Final Notice' stamped in red across the top. And a gas bill, another final demand letter. And one for the TV licence. Frantic, Mam stuffed them back into her bag.

I sat down again.

The words 'Final Notice' were cemented in my brain.

Things had reached breaking point.

I pulled out my phone and sent Finn a quick text:

Give Clint the nod

Straight away, Finn replied:

Savage

Later on, Finn sent me a link to where he'd posted the video of Clint's madcap attempts to scale the fence. Like a crazed animal trying to escape its pen.

The video already had hundreds of hits. Not so bad.

26
TRICKY DOHERTY

'Who's the sham?'

Finn nodded towards a bushy type, leaning against Paddy Tarantino's shed, smoking and spitting.

Paddy shifted about on his feet. 'Shay Doherty. TT's da.'

I flinched. More banana-skin territory. 'What's going on, Paddy?'

'Bit of an issue.'

He threw daggers at the old guy.

'Yeah?' I said anxiously.

'Turns out Da still owes Mr Doherty here cash for the piglets.'

'So?' said Finn eventually. 'Just pay the dude. I don't see what the big deal is.'

I raised my eyebrows at Paddy. I wasn't clear on the implications either.

'So, legally, Mr Doherty still owns two-thirds of these pigs. The pigs that I've – no, sorry, we've – made a fortune from. Picture getting any clearer?'

Finn looked horrified. 'Hold on, you're not suggesting that … that this … this hobo thinks he's entitled to a pay-off?'

Paddy winced. 'Worse. Not only has he added a couple of hundred to the original price of the pigs – to take into account their earning potential –'

I took a breath, waiting for the sting.

'– but he wants a cut of the earnings. Past and future.'

'What?' Finn hissed. 'There's no way.'

Paddy cut him off. 'Hello. This is a Doherty we're talking about. They're trouble.'

'Don't we know!' I cut in.

'He's already hinted to Da about settin' their dogs on his sheep. No point in messin' with 'em.'

'What about legally?' Finn said.

Paddy laughed. 'Legally, the Dohertys are one step ahead. Shay's already threatened Da with a letter. Some fifteenth cousin of his is a solicitor. You know what they're like.'

I looked up. 'Seriously?'

'Not so much of a sham now, is he? More clever than he looks.'

Finn scowled, clenching his fists. 'Surely we can talk to him. Offer to pay a good price for the pigs and his cut of the action.'

'Nope, Finn. You don't reason with the Dohertys. This one here's a mad man. Probably has a shotgun in the van.'

'Paddy's right. I don't think we've much choice but to pay up.'

Finn nodded glumly. 'How much is this gonna cost us?'

'Too much for my liking. I'm afraid that's the end of the pig videos. I'm out,' said Paddy.

'What? Feck sake, Paddy, you can't be serious,' Finn exclaimed.

Paddy shook his head resolutely. 'It's not worth the sweat. Not when I've to cough up a few hundred extra for the pigs to get Shay off Da's back. And then split any earnings from the vids three ways.'

'So what are you sayin', Paddy?' said Finn.

'I'm not doing business with Shay Doherty, that's what I'm sayin'.'

'Well, neither are we,' I said quickly. Especially as we already had TT Doherty chasing us down. The very last thing I wanted was another Doherty rocking up to my front door. 'We'll have to sell the pigs back to him.'

'And cut our losses,' Paddy said. 'Exactly.'

Finn almost choked. 'What? Jaysus, lads, you're killin' me.'

Finn pulled me to one side. 'This is a big mistake. Colossal.'

'We've no choice, Finn,' I said. For once, I needed to stand my ground. 'And don't exaggerate.'

'Tu. Tu.'

'Tu. Tu.'

'What's that bloody noise?' Finn said, still steaming.

'Tu. Tu.'

'Tu. Tu.'

Shay Doherty was slouched over, spitting furiously. Then I noticed he'd a dog with him. A large black Rottweiler, drool dripping liberally from his mouth and forming a puddle on the ground.

'What's it to be, lads?'

Paddy spoke. 'Mr Doherty, sir, we'd like to sell you back the pigs.'

Finn and I exchanged glances. Sir. Paddy was laying it on thick.

Shay Doherty snorted. 'Would you indeed. Ha! You'd like to sell me back me own pigs. That's a good one, wha' you think,

Tricky?' He rubbed the top of the dog's head affectionately. The dog whimpered and rolled on its back.

'Here's what's gonna happen, lads.' Shay pointed at Paddy. 'Firstly, Mr Hollywood here is gonna pay me the money I'm owed on the pigs.'

Tricky yapped in agreement.

Shay grinned, arms outstretched. 'Then we're all gonna go into business together. I'm an honest man, when all is said'n' done. A two-way split: seventy for me, and thirty for you lot.'

'Wait, you said fifty–fifty,' Paddy said.

Shay held his hand up. 'Let's not fall out now, boy. Seventy–thirty is a fair split. Generous, I'd say, given me lost earnings so far.'

Finn spluttered loudly. 'Lost earnings. Are you off your rocker?'

Tricky stood up on all fours, growling, and made a lunge at Finn, held back only by Shay grabbing his collar.

'Lads, come on, we're not accepting this, right?' Finn said, bending down to tie his lace that had loosened.

Tricky escaped his master's grip. He bounded forward and head-butted Finn with his snout, bang on the forehead.

'What the –?' Finn cried, thrown to the ground.

Shay whistled for the dog, who ran over to his side. He rubbed Tricky's stomach. 'C'mere girl. She's excitable, is Tricky.'

Finn rubbed the top of his head, dazed.

Carefully, I sidestepped over to Finn, keeping one eye on the dog. I helped him to his feet, muttering in his ear: 'I get the distinct impression that this isn't exactly a proposal that you can chew over and come back with a counter-offer on.'

Paddy nodded, joining us. 'Luke's right, Finn, ya mad buck.

Nobody takes on a Doherty. Let's just call it quits and get rid for now.'

I glanced over to where Shay Doherty stood, carefully picking his nose. Paddy was dead right. Stamping our feet was no use. We'd need to out-manoeuvre Shay Doherty with a sharper piece of play.

'Right so, business partners. I'll be off. Say goodbye, Tricky.'

Tricky snarled in our direction.

'One more thing, young fellas.'

Reluctantly, we turned back around.

'I hear you've also got a little project on the go with TT, me youngest. He's a smart lad. Gifted with a similar business brain to mine.'

'He's kept that talent well hidden,' Finn said quietly.

Shay shuffled into his van, with Tricky curled up in the passenger seat. He poked his head out the driver's window. 'Be in your interest to stay on the right side of TT. Then you stay on the right side of me, got it?'

That sounded like a veiled threat.

The van skidded on the gravel and sped off.

Finn sighed loudly. 'Feck sake, lads. Double Dohertys. Can things get any worse?'

I saw the beginnings of a nasty purple bruise forming right in the middle of Finn's forehead.

But I kept my mouth shut.

27

QUIVERS QUINN

Clint pointed towards the goal. 'Lads, I'm telling yis, this shootout ain't goin' ahead until that penalty spot is sorted.'

'What's the problem?' Emily asked Clint, all business-like.

'I can't bleedin' see it.'

Finn nudged me. 'Luke, go over and take a look.'

I jogged over. Clint had a point. No circle, just a tiny white sliver of grass.

'Somebody get the spray and sort it now,' Finn ordered, flexing his hands, agitated.

Gabe nodded and ran off in the direction of the caretaker's shed.

Koby appeared. 'Speedy's not happy,' he reported.

We all looked over to the far side of the pitch where Speedy was frantically doing press-ups, probably for the fun of it. Or to impress the growing crowd.

Finn threw his arms up. 'What is it now?'

'He's complaining that Quivers Quinn isn't fit.'

Finn sighed loudly. 'Tough. Tell him Quivers is the only goalie we have.'

I handed Koby a chocolate bar. 'Give this to Speedy. He's probably famished. Should tide him over.'

Finn snorted. 'We'll never get this thing started. Where is Quivers, by the way?'

Emily looked at her watch. 'He's probably on his way over now. He's in detention all this week. Some scrap in the canteen.'

Finn rolled his eyes.

Clint reappeared and slapped Finn on the back, who toppled over from the force of it. 'All righ', Fitzy, I'm happy enough with the penalty spot. Gabe's sorted it. Top man is Gabe.'

'No problemo, Clint boy,' Gabe said, happily spraying all around him with the white spray can. He drew around Finn, sprawled on the grass, as if he were a dead body.

Finn hopped up and grabbed the can. 'Gabe, quit messin' about.'

Clint started to giggle. 'Yis are a riot.'

'Can you go and warm up?' said Finn to Clint impatiently.

'Lads, sorry I'm late.'

Emily stifled a laugh. 'Well, shiver me timbers, it's Quivers.'

I frowned and turned to see Quivers jogging towards us, togged out in his gear but wearing an oversized black patch over his right eye. 'Quivers, good to see you. What's the story with the patch?'

Quivers said, 'Bog Buckley threw his phone at me. Corner of it caught me eyeball. Spent a night in A&E.'

I squirmed. 'Nasty.'

'What did you do to deserve that?' said Finn.

'According to Bog, I skipped the queue in the canteen. And took the last sausage.'

'Bog is a wild man. Some temper on him,' I acknowledged, with some sympathy for Quivers.

'You look ridiculous, by the way,' said Emily, blunt as ever, biting her lip. 'Where'd you get that patch?'

Quivers shrugged. 'It's for a horse. Only one I could find.'

'Ahoy, matey. Who's this spanner?' said Clint, giving Quivers the once-over.

'This is Quivers, our goalie,' Finn said. 'Quivers, this is Clint, our super sub.'

Quivers nodded at Clint.

Clint took a step back, digesting this information. He rubbed his eyes, like he was seeing things. 'Hold it, bud. Hold it righ' there. Are you seriously tellin' me tha' we're usin' a one-eyed goalie? A bleedin' one-eyed goalie.'

'He has a point,' said Emily, laughing, despite heated looks from Finn.

Clint tapped his head. 'This is a joke, righ'? Yis are havin' a laugh wit me, righ', Fitzy?'

Finn looked fit to burst. The pressure was getting to him.

'What's your problem, buck?' Quivers said, suddenly realising the joke was on him. He took a threatening step towards Clint.

I put my hand out to intervene. 'Clint, Quivers is a top goalie, with or without the use of both his eyes. Won the "Outstanding Player of the Year" award at our club. Great hands.'

'And he made a few top class peno saves last season,' Finn added.

I nodded. 'You won't get one past him that easily.'

'Lightning quick,' said Finn, overcooking it.

Clint opened his eyes wide. He glared at Quivers, unconvinced. 'All righ', I'll take yer word for it.'

He picked up the ball and spun it in his hand, still watching Quivers out of the corner of his eye, muttering away. 'A bleedin' one-eyed goalie. Wait'll I tell the lads back home – they'll wet themselves.'

Koby arrived over with Speedy in tow.

'Right, let's get this party started,' said Finn.

He fished in his pocket for a coin.

Finn turned to Speedy. 'Heads or tails?'

Speedy was pacing furiously, not paying attention.

Finn gave up and turned to Clint. 'Heads or tails, cuz?'

'Heads, bud.'

Finn tossed the coin. 'Tails.' He spent a few minutes attempting to grab hold of Speedy. 'Speedy, quit moving. You're up first.'

Suddenly, there was a loud eruption of hoots and wolf whistles.

'Get a load of those pins.'

'Nice tan, baby.'

'Rockin' those legs.'

'Fake-tan fail.'

'What now?' said Finn, face like thunder.

'Ho-ho, it's Clint. He's down to his shorts,' I said, nodding towards the goal line. Clint had removed his pants to reveal bright orange-streaked legs underneath. It was causing quite a stir, especially amongst all the girls that had gathered behind the goal.

'Oompa Loompa doompa-dee-do,' Emily sang.

Finn stalked over. 'Clint, mate, what's with the legs?'

Clint beamed proudly. 'Ah, yeah, like 'em? Goin' on me holliers in a few weeks, Fitzy. Prep for me beach look.'

Finn sniffed. 'What's that smell?'

'Got a great deal on the tanning oil, great deal altogether. Home-made, it is.'

Clint waved enthusiastically into the crowd.

I followed his gaze. There stood Mona Lisa Murphy, waving coyly back at Clint, clearly one of her many satisfied customers.

Clint wrinkled his nose. 'One major problem: the stench. Mouldy. The stuff reeks, it does. Reeks of coffee.'

Emily nearly lost her life. 'This is too much. I'm weak. My ribs are actually sore from laughing.'

Slowly, Finn strolled back over to us. 'This is a farce.' He put his hands over his face. 'It's turning into a complete and utter joke.'

I couldn't really disagree with him. 'Let's crack on.'

Finn blew his whistle to kick things off. Quivers took centre stage in the goal.

Speedy stepped up to take his first penalty.

The crowd chanted 'Speed-y, Speed-y, Speed-y', but hushed as soon as Speedy stepped back from the penalty spot.

BANG.

1-0.

Quivers didn't get near it.

Next up, Clint danced over to the goal, punching the air, like he was a boxer in the ring.

'He's psyching himself up,' said Finn knowingly.

Responding to the spontaneous applause, Clint threw his hands up in the air, like a superstar.

Carefully, he placed the ball down on the spot.

'The crowd is really gettin' going,' Koby shouted.

'That's cos everyone has money on this,' I said.

Clint chipped the ball into the right corner.

1-1.

I spotted TT Doherty skulking at the back of the crowd. He caught me looking at him. Quickly, I turned back to the action, hoping that he wouldn't come over. Finn was already wound up enough.

Speedy pounced onto the penalty spot, revved up and fired the ball neatly into the top corner.

Clint sprang up. 'The whistle. Ref, he needs to wait for the bleedin' whistle. They're the rules.'

Speedy's eyes darted from Clint to Finn. 'I heard a whistle.'

'Maybe in your head, bud. There was no whistle,' said Clint, agitated, turning to Finn. 'Tell him.'

'Take it again, Speedy,' Finn said, blowing on the whistle sharply.

Rattled, Speedy miskicked the ball, but it still rolled softly past Quivers and plopped into the net.

2-1.

'Quivers is useless,' Finn said, turning away.

'Be fair, he is operating with just one eye,' I said. 'Plus, he's distracted. He keeps fiddling with that patch.'

Finn snorted. 'He didn't even get a hand to that one.'

'Sure, poor Quivers has to shield his good eye from the blinding rays,' I said.

'What rays? Look up. Grey clouds. And more grey clouds –'

I pointed to the far side, where Clint was studiously stretching his hamstrings. 'No, the ultraviolet radiation being emitted from Clint's glow-in-the-dark pins.'

'State of him. He's a radioactive disaster waitin' to happen, that lad. Bloody Mona Lisa and her knock-off potions.'

Next up, it was Clint's turn in the spotlight. He made a run at the ball but stopped dead mid-kick, instead pointing at Quivers in disgust. 'No way, I'm not havin' it. He's off his goal line. Look at him. He's miles away from the line. Does anyone play by the rules around here, wha'?'

He had a point. Quivers was flailing around in front of the goal like a sick puppy, flapping his arms, way off his line.

Finn let out a roar. 'Quivers, get the hell back.'

Clint positioned the ball on the penalty spot again. But he was interrupted by growing protests from the throngs of people packed tight behind the goal. Quivers had bobbed over the goal line again, waving his hands in the air like a demented dancing puppet, eye glazed over.

Finn whacked his forehead. 'Jaysus, what's got into Quivers? He's lost it.'

Clint turned to us, his short fuse getting shorter by the second. 'It's a bleedin' set-up this. Mind games. Your pirate boy's playin' dirty tricks. Hoppin' around the place like a drunken chicken, tryin' to put me off.'

The crowd reacted aggressively on both sides: those with bets on Clint to win hissing and booing at Quivers's alleged distraction tactics, and those with bets on Speedy whooping and jeering.

I nudged Finn, sensing the growing unease. 'We need to get a handle on this.'

Finn coaxed Clint back to the penalty spot.

Meanwhile, I tried to get through to Quivers, who seemed oblivious, gently shoving him back behind the goal line. 'Quivers, mate, keep calm. See the white line? You gotta stand on it, right?' I caught hold of his arms and dragged them down to his sides.

Eventually, Clint jogged over to take his penalty. He whacked the ball with such force, I thought it might burst the net. Quivers didn't stand a chance, on or off the goal line.

2-2.

Speedy stepped up. He scuffed the grass a few times, then managed to get a foot to the ball.

3-2.

Clint protested immediately. 'Whoa, whoa, ya chancer. Fake kick. Fake kick.'

Speedy frowned, eyes twitching.

'You country boys haven't read the poxy rule book. You can't fake kick the ball,' said Clint, furious.

Speedy took a swig of his energy drink. 'Eh, legitimate kick, that was, buck.'

I felt the fumes emanating from Clint. 'He's gonna blow.'

And right on cue, Clint made a sudden lunge for Speedy. I darted over and, together with Finn, managed to haul Clint away before he mauled Speedy to pieces.

The crowd were growing increasingly restless and threatening, having gradually moved in tighter and tighter around the goal area.

Finn blew the whistle to try to calm the situation. 'Right, Speedy, I'm dockin' you a point for that zinger. Score's back to 2-2. Clint, you're up.'

Speedy's head vibrated, probably trying to process this information.

'Jeez, for such a headcase, he's a stickler for the rules, is our Clint,' said Finn into my ear, tutting.

Clint was riled. The tension was palpable. He placed the ball on the grass. I noticed he took a few seconds longer to put the ball on the penalty spot, rolling it around.

WHACK.

Quivers was awake for this one and, by some miracle, he guessed the correct side. He dived to the right and managed to get a touch on the ball. It swerved to the right of the goal, narrowly avoiding the post.

The crowd went crazy, resulting in a pitch invasion.

Clint froze. His cheeks fizzed up until they were neon red. He stampeded at Quivers like a raging bull, plastering him up against the goalpost. 'Wha' was that all abou', bud?'

There was a hush, except for the odd person shouting, 'Fight! Fight!'

'What?' said Quivers, trying to breathe.

'Whadaya mean, what? You barely bleedin' moved, like a poxy statue, up to now.'

'I dunno what your problem is –' Quivers started.

'And then, bam, all of a sudden, you hop up like a bleedin' cocker spaniel to save my penalty,' Clint said, spitting through his teeth.

'You need to c-calm d-d-down, dude,' Quivers stuttered.

'Don't tell me what to do, pirate boy.'

Clint picked Quivers up by the ears. Next minute, the ball, fired in from the crowd, smashed Quivers square in the face. Quivers's good eye rolled back into its socket and he fainted.

And just like that, the party was over.

'What the hell is going on?' I jumped on hearing TT Doherty's voice. He reefed Clint up by the T-shirt and pointed to Quivers, passed out on the grass. 'We're down a goalie cos of you, joker. Best out of five penos is the deal here.'

It was bad timing on TT's part. Clint, wound up like a tight spring until now, finally reached his breaking point and erupted. Without warning, he body-slammed TT, blasting him across the ground.

Next minute, Clint was squatting, with the goal hoisted high above his shoulders.

'Feck sake, Clint. Put that down,' Finn yelled.

Clint stood up quickly and straightened out his arms, like he was a super-heavyweight at the Olympics. He dropped the goal on top of TT, trapping him inside the net.

Clint punched his chest in satisfaction. 'Who's the bleedin' joke now, country boy, eh?'

I watched in fascination as TT desperately tried to disentangle himself from the net, like a fly attempting to escape a spider's web. People surrounded the goal, mocking his pathetic attempts to lift the goalposts and crawl out.

'Maybe we should get Clint outta here?' I said, sensing the already-high pressure building.

Finn nodded and stalked over to sweet-talk him.

$ $ $

It later transpired that Quivers was dosed up on potent painkillers for his gammy eye and was clearly still feeling the side-effects. We were lucky he could stand, never mind stop a ball. That explained the demented puppet act too.

'Poor Quivers. Fainting on the job. His goalkeeping rep is in tatters,' said Finn, chuckling.

'Quivers was a victim. I told you that Clint was a loose one.'

Finn sighed. 'That's what you get when you pay peanuts.'

My eyes widened. 'What are you talkin' about? You told me Clint was a friend of the family.'

Finn threw me a look. 'Cop on, Luke. Don't play dumb. I hired him, obviously.'

'What?'

'Yeah. Just made a few inquiries. Got him from a footie contact in the city.'

I rubbed the perspiration from my forehead. 'Well, that was a clever move. Hiring a complete maniac.'

'Had you any better ideas at the time? No, I didn't think so.'

'It's a financial massacre.' I sighed. 'TT's stinging us for all the refunds. All bets are voided because we didn't finish the shootout. We never got to the five penalties.'

'We'll have to keep a low profile next few days. Avoid TT Doherty until we can round up the cash.'

I pictured TT's face, humiliated, as he clambered out from under that football net.

Once he caught up with us, we were going to be toast.

28

POWDER KEANE

'One: a ruptured football net, for which I expect to be recompensed. Two: Mr Quinn, admitted to A&E for facial trauma – a fractured cheekbone, to be precise. Not to mind the fact he was found lying unconscious on the pitch. Three: running an illegal betting exchange on school premises.

'No.' Powder raised his hand. 'Don't say a word, Mr Fitzpatrick. Not until you're asked.

'Four: I've just had the principal of St Joseph's College on the phone. There's been a serious incident linked to a phone app called Tagged. This app seems to originate from this school. Five: there is also an accusation of infiltrating the IT system at Josephs.'

Powder rechecked his notes, lips puckered. Satisfied that he'd covered all bases, he leaned across the table, his enormous torso towering over us, his chunky fingers drumming the desk. 'Where to start, eh, gentlemen? You have been busy.'

Slowly, he squished himself down into his chair, reached for his mug and hoovered up the tea, taking care not to spill it down his brown corduroy suit, all the while watching us.

We sat there in torturous silence for at least five mouthfuls of tea.

Powder straightened his tie. 'Would you like to hear more?'

I went to open my mouth, but my tongue was wedged firmly to its roof.

Finn nodded mutely.

Powder shuffled his notes. 'Apparently, this incident involved a fake profile on the Tagged app, which was used as a smokescreen for a house party, where considerable damage was done to the property.'

Beside me, I could feel Finn tense. A fake profile. So much for the Sullivans' cast-iron code.

'People were able to confirm their attendance at the house party using the LIKE button. The fake profile spread like wildfire.' Powder eyeballed us over the notes. 'You can see where this is going, right, gentlemen?'

I gulped.

'So many people turned up to the party, it descended into total chaos. The place was trashed, and the guards were called.'

I gulped again, louder.

But Powder wasn't finished. 'And the guards are now investigating this incident, following the trail all the way back to – yeah, you guessed it, this app.'

Powder sat back, flexing his fingers, letting his words sink in.

'Mysteriously, every student ID number for St Josephs College ended up on a list here. The caretaker found it discarded in the bin.'

I closed my eyes briefly. That was just carelessness by the Sullivans. No excuses. Of course, with no Koby around to monitor them, they were bound to go off-road eventually. Leaving us as roadkill.

I shut my eyes and waited for the roasting.

It wasn't a long wait.

Powder surged towards us and slammed the notepad down hard, causing the desk to vibrate.

We shrank back into our chairs.

'This has your name written all over it, Fitzpatrick. And your henchmen here.' Powder clenched his jaw, swinging his thick neck from side to side, like a bullock. 'I know that you prize idiots are connected to all this. Consider yourselves very, very fortunate. Right now, I can't pin any of this on you, except damaging school property. But if I get even a sniff of evidence …'

I watched as a long cheese-like string of drool that had been lingering from the side of Powder's mouth finally splashed onto the table with a plop.

Powder wiped his face. 'You're getting off lightly with just two weeks' detention and lunchtime litter duty.'

I slumped forward, wiping my forehead in relief. Sounded like Powder wasn't going to ring our parents. The last thing Mam needed was a Powder blast down the phone.

Plus it seemed Miss Shine hadn't blabbed to Powder about our alleged involvement with the app. Not yet anyway. That singing deal with Pablo was keeping her at bay. Plus a lack of hard evidence.

Powder thumped the punchbag hanging in the middle of his office, sending it flying in our direction. We jerked out of the way.

Powder jabbed his finger in our faces. 'You're on my radar. One more close shave with me and it'll be straight to suspension. And your parents will be called in. Got it?'

He indicated towards the door.

'The app, sir?' Finn piped up.

'What about it?' said Powder.

Finn squirmed in his chair.

Powder hummed. 'Ah, that's right. The app is an item on the school-council agenda tonight. I'll contact them and tell them not to bother. The app is history. You'd hardly think that I'd allow it to go to a council vote now. Not after this business with St Josephs.'

My stomach churned. The app was our most dependable source of cash. Wiped out in a flash. That awkward negotiating with Katy Doyle, all for nothing. And the Sullivans were about to embark on the design of Tagged 2.0.

Powder took another swing at the punchbag. 'We're damn lucky the TV crew haven't got wind of this.'

$ $ $

Finn pointed to a shadowy figure scuttling around the street corner. 'That's bloody Mulgrew. C'mon, let's get after him.'

I tugged at his coat. 'Forget about Lochy Mulgrew. We've bigger problems.'

Finn blew me off. 'No way. He's the one got us into this mess with TT Doherty. And then did a vanishing act.'

'Cop on, Finn, we should never have got involved with Lochy. We knew he was bad news.'

'Lochy should've told us that TT Doherty had him by the short 'n' curlies.'

'No. We should've done our homework on him,' I said, turning to walk up the street.

Finn's phone beeped.

He caught up with me after a minute.

'TT. He wants to see us today.'

I froze. 'For what?'

'How do I know?'

I bit my fingernail. 'But we don't have the cash yet.'

Finn refocused, eyes bloodshot. 'We'll have to buy some time.'

I considered the titanic prospect of negotiating with TT. 'Finn, he'll be like a hyena on steroids after being trapped under that goal.'

Finn chewed this over. 'Not much choice.'

Suddenly, I felt slightly queasy and reached out to Finn's shoulder to balance myself.

'Jaysus, look at the bloody state of us. Nervous wrecks.' Finn kicked the wall, nearly toppling me over. 'First TT Doherty. And now we've pit-bull Powder sniffin' around too.'

'Calm it, Finn.'

His outburst was attracting attention.

'You absolutely sure about Mulgrew? From where I'm standing, revenge sounds pretty sweet,' Finn said, spitting. 'It'll certainly make me feel a whole lot better.'

29
THE STAG BEETLE

TT raised the lid of the lunchbox.

'Ugh, what's that?'

TT slammed his phone torch directly into Finn's face. 'Wha' does it look like, genius?'

I peered over Finn's shoulder. 'A big beetle?'

TT gently poked its curved horns with his finger, triggering a frenzied bolt around the sides of the box, similar to a cyclist in a velodrome. 'This ain't just any beetle. It's a stag beetle.'

'Nice,' Finn muttered.

'Valuable insect you're lookin' at.'

TT wedged a piece of squished plum into the lunchbox.

'Worth a fortune, this one, because of its extra-long horns.'

TT shut the lid tight, securing the sides. The beetle rammed its horns against the plastic. 'He's a cocky one, this guy. You'll see that. Likes smashin' up his horns. Showin' off.'

Finn flashed me a look. Neither of us said anything. I wasn't sure where this was going. TT was acting strange – not friendly, but not his usual hostile, intimidating self.

Unnerving was an understatement.

TT thrust the lunchbox in Finn's direction. 'Don't worry, he won't bite. Well, not unless he's hungry.'

Finn sprang back, but TT gripped his arm roughly and enclosed the lunchbox in his other hand.

'These beetles can get dehydrated, so keep him somewhere shaded, like under a bed.' TT picked up the shopping bag at his feet and handed it to me. 'He needs to be fed once a day.'

I looked down at the contents. Fruit. And more fruit.

'TT, eh, I might be missin' something,' Finn said, one eye on the lunchbox. 'But why are you tellin' us all this?'

All the while, Finn kept his arm outstretched, like he was holding a poisonous snake. The beetle was still hurtling madly around the container, wrestling noisily with itself.

TT slapped Finn on the cheeks. 'Because, pretty boy, you're gonna be mindin' it for the week.'

Finn's face shuddered. 'Wha'? But –'

'This isn't up for negotiation.'

Finn sniffed. 'But I've a phobia of bugs – well, spiders.'

TT jabbed the lunchbox. 'Does that look like a spider to you, clown? The guards are sniffin' around our gaff. It's to do with the brothers.'

Suddenly, the beetle stopped moving, throwing the street into total silence.

'The guards?' I said, louder than I'd planned.

TT scowled, putting his finger to his lips. 'Shut it. The whole world doesn't need to know.'

Finn glared at me.

'Sorry,' I mouthed.

'I need to keep that little guy away from pryin' eyes, just until the court case is over,' TT said, nodding at the lunchbox.

Court case.

I dropped the shopping bag with a bang. That rumour about TT's brothers being charged with handling counterfeit goods wasn't off the mark then.

The fruit scattered over the road, like balls breaking on a snooker table.

TT flared his nostrils, infuriated. He bent down and scooped up a peach in each hand. Coolly, he stepped towards us, trapping us at the wall and hustling in uncomfortably close.

'You owe me. All that messin' with the goalie, trust me, you're gettin' away lightly.'

He raised his hands and mashed the peaches down on the top of our heads, compressing the fruit until the stone grazed our skulls and juice ran down our faces.

Then he squeezed his sticky hands tight around our necks.

Tighter.

Tighter.

Tighter.

Until my throat was choked and I could barely breathe.

Abruptly, TT released us. 'I want the cash to cover the bet refunds by the weekend. All of it. The punters are gettin' a bit restless.'

He nodded towards the lunchbox. 'And I want that beetle back in exactly the same condition. You need to handle that creature like it's a newborn baby. And do not remove it from that container. It has special ventilation holes to keep it alive. Got it?'

We nodded mutely.

TT's eyes flashed. 'Oh, I almost forgot, a friendly message from my da. He's not one bit happy with those celebrity pigs.

Says that your mate Paddy isn't makin' any effort to promote them any more. And there's been no new videos. Says he's been round to see Paddy more than once to try and sort it.'

I winced. Poor Paddy. Sounded like he was being harassed by Shay Doherty.

Finn blew out his cheeks noisily.

TT eyeballed him. 'You got a problem?'

Finn coughed. 'No, no. Just not sure what we can do.'

TT surged forward and reefed Finn up by the ears. 'You bucks need to persuade your mate to start promoting them pigs, otherwise Da'll come knockin' on your door.'

After one final check on the beetle, TT stalked off.

'He's septic,' I muttered, watching him disappear out of sight.

'He's a complete maniac.'

Finn placed the lunchbox on the roof of a nearby parked car, sat down on the kerb and massaged the back of his neck. After a minute, he became engrossed in the task of trying to extract the sticky peach paste from his hair.

I scurried about, retrieving the bruised fruit.

'Finn,' I roared, pointing at the car.

The box had slid down the roof and was dangling precariously off the side. Finn pounced and caught it just in time.

'Here,' he said, passing the box to me.

I threw up my hands. 'Why are you giving it to me?'

Finn scrunched his nose up. 'But you're takin' it, right?'

I pushed the box away. 'No way. You're taking it.'

'C'mon, Luke, you know I've got arra … phobia.'

'You mean arachnophobia?

'Yeah, yeah, that's it.'

'It's a beetle, Finn, not a flippin' black widow.'

'Please, Luke. You know I'm useless at looking after things. Remember Lisa Simpson?'

I pictured Lisa Simpson, Finn's pet budgie, found lying on her back in her cage, legs up in the air, completely unresponsive.

I rolled my eyes, reluctantly offering a hand for the box.

'You know it makes sense,' said Finn.

30

THE REVOLUTIONARY

'Take a look.'

I gazed into the old butcher's shop window, pressing my nose against the polished glass.

'When?'

Finn ran his hands through his hair. 'No idea. One day it's empty. The next day – this. A nail salon.'

There was a knock at the window. I leapt away.

'Luke, we have to get the butcher's block from under those floorboards. Otherwise, we can kiss goodbye to any hope of getting rid of TT Doherty.'

'And that's assuming the money's still there.'

'Don't even think like that. All our feckin' cash is in that block,' Finn howled.

'All of it?'

'Pretty much. Excluding the emergency cash I gave to Pablo.'

I studied Finn's face for a moment. It was the first time I'd seen him panicked. TT Doherty had really got to him. To both of us.

'Stupid question, but you checked the keys, right?'

'Feck sake. Of course. All the locks have been changed.'

'Does your mam have a key?'

Finn exhaled noisily. 'I already went through her big bundle of work keys. No joy.'

'How're we gonna get into the salon? Any ideas?'

Finn looked around. 'Yeah, but we really need Gabe.'

'Really? Would Emily not be better?'

'No, Emily's such a nose. She'll want to know everything, review all the finer details of the plan. Trust me. Gabe's our only option.'

'Speak of the devil.'

Gabe appeared, dressed head to toe in khaki military gear, complete with bright pink headphones blaring. 'HOWAYA LADS. NEW DANCE ALBUM. EPIC.'

Finn popped up one of the earpads. 'Gabe, mate, you're yelling.'

Gabe pulled off the headphones.

'Nice headgear,' said Finn, nodding at the oversized army cap.

I whistled. 'What's with the outfit?'

'Lads, remember this day. It's the day I decided to become a revolution-ary.'

Finn arched his eyebrow. 'Yeah, fair play. What's the deal then?'

'Huh?'

'What are you planning to do, exactly? As a revolutionary?'

Gabe clenched his fists. 'I'm joining the rebellion, the uprising.'

I patted his back. 'Admirable, Gabe. Not many of them around these parts, though.'

'When did this revolutionary calling happen?'

'I dreamt about it last night.'

'Stuff of nightmares,' I muttered. 'Gabe in an army.'

'Gabe, show me your hands,' Finn ordered, changing the subject.

Gabe stood there, immobile.

'Your hands,' Finn repeated impatiently, grabbing one of Gabe's arms roughly.

Gabe held out his hands, palms facing up.

Finn turned them around and examined his nails. 'Bit mucky. But otherwise, they'll do.'

'Do for what?'

Finn read the menu taped to the window. 'Hmm ... the mini-manicure, I think.'

'Gabe?' I said, sceptically.

'Yeah, it's the cheapest and it's thirty minutes long. Plenty of time for distractions.'

We tripped into the nail salon, followed by Gabe, who seemed to be none the wiser.

'A mini-manicure for my friend here,' said Finn to the girl at the desk, pointing to Gabe. He slapped down a bundle of ten-euro notes.

The girl glanced up from filing her nails. She shot Gabe a look that could kill. 'Take a seat there.'

Finn shoved Gabe into the chair.

'Rita,' the girl called. 'One for you.'

Rita, a short, middle-aged woman, complete with an extraordinary high lilac beehive, appeared at the stairs, already donning a disapproving look. 'What do you want, boys?'

'One mini-mani, please.'

'Is this a joke?' She picked up the sweeping brush and tried to shoo us towards the door. 'This is a respectable salon. Out you go.'

'What? But we've already paid,' Finn protested.

Rita turned to the desk girl, who simply shrugged and continued filing. 'All right then, but you two need to wait outside.'

Finn's face fell. Not part of the plan, I guessed.

'Can't we just sit over there?' I said.

'We'll be quiet, I swear,' said Finn.

Eventually, Rita gave in. We skulked over to the corner and picked up a magazine each, ignoring the stares from the other customers.

Rita barked at Gabe, who looked like a rabbit in headlights. 'Polish?'

No reaction.

'What colour polish do you want?' she said, noticing Gabe's android expression.

Gabe sat back and thought hard about her question. Really hard. Actually considered it, like it was the most important decision he'd need to make that day.

Rita was fit to burst.

'Black, and red for my thumbs,' Gabe said finally.

When Rita disappeared to get Gabe's preferred nail polish, and with the reception girl still filing furiously, Finn took his chance and slipped over behind the till to the loose floorboards. I watched him from above my magazine, speculating on what plan he'd hatched. Stooped, he slipped a package out from under his jacket, but spun around then, obstructing my view. Within seconds, he was back in his chair, looking more relaxed.

'Sorted,' he said, winking at me. 'Just watch and learn, Lukey. Watch and learn.'

Meanwhile, back at planet Gabe, Rita was regaling him with some animated tale while faffing around with his cuticles. Gabe looked genuinely engaged in conversation. Bizarre.

'You wanna upgrade to the deluxe manicure for an extra tenner, sweetie?' Rita cooed.

'Eh, no, he doesn't, thanks,' Finn piped up loudly from across the room. He turned to me. 'Huh, it's sweetie now. Gabe could become a regular in here.'

'Anything going to happen yet?' I whispered, after the longest two minutes in history.

'Give it a sec,' Finn said. 'Trust me, this is the calm before the storm.'

Another minute went by.

Finn nudged me. 'How's the beetle?'

'Still alive.'

'When did you last check?'

'This morning.'

'And you're feedin' it?'

'Yes. Quit hounding me.'

'Luke, that beetle is the Kanye West of beetles. Rock-star treatment the whole way. In fact, that beetle could be our white flag in this war with TT Doherty.'

I didn't respond, thinking back to the shrivelled piece of plum I'd thrown in the lunchbox earlier. I'd better check on it later.

Eventually, I couldn't stand it. 'What exactly are we waiting for?'

'Patience, Lukey. Patience.' Finn closed his eyes. 'Come on, baby, come on.'

'RAT. RAAAT. RAAAAAAT!' The reception girl let out a series of glass-shattering shrieks and scrambled up onto her chair.

Panic ensued.

Poor Rita's hair nearly subsided as she made a dash for it. Gabe wasn't far behind her, I noted. Followed by the receptionist, who was hysterical at this point. She clawed at her legs repeatedly, claiming that the rat had rubbed up against them.

Within minutes, the shop had emptied.

We legged it across the floor, and I pulled up the loose floorboard.

'Bingo,' said Finn, reaching for the butcher's block.

'The money?'

'It's all there. We're good,' Finn replied, breathing a huge sigh of relief. He flung his gear bag at me. 'Wait here.'

I stuffed the piles of money into the bag.

Within minutes, Finn returned, thrusting a brown envelope towards my chest. 'Here. I forgot all about Mucker's tickets. The Golden Tickets.'

I shoved the envelope into my pocket. 'Let's go.'

'Wait, I just need to get Betty.'

'Who's Betty?'

'Paddy's pet gopher.'

'But that girl thought it was a rat.'

'We sprayed her dark brown, for effect,' Finn said. 'Ah, here she is, and she ate her berries.'

The gopher bounded towards Finn and snuggled into her pouch.

$ $ $

'Did you know Rita used to work behind the counter at the supermarket? She said she recognised me from all the breakfast rolls I used to buy.'

I smothered a grin.

'They wanted her to cut her crazy hair, so she quit and started up the salon,' Gabe said excitedly.

'Sounds like you got the whole story,' I said, raising my eyebrows at Finn.

'Sound woman, Rita. Awful pity about her rat invasion,' Gabe lamented.

'Yeah, it's a real shame,' Finn said, wrinkling his nose.

'So, Gabe, I didn't realise you were an AC Milan fan?' I said, pointing at his half-manicured red and black nails.

'No, these are the colours of my hero: Che Guevara. A true revolutionary.'

'What's that in your hand?' I said, spotting a bottle.

'It's moisturiser, to keep my hands and nails silky smooth. Rita gave it to me.'

Finn slapped him on the back. 'I'm sure Che would be so proud.'

31
UFO

'Hold it. Where're you off to at this hour?'

Dad's head appeared around the front door.

I skulked back up the driveway. 'Just round to Finn's.'

He crossed his arms and leaned against the doorframe. 'Speaking of Finn, I bumped into Mrs Fitzpatrick in town the other day.'

I edged backwards. 'Oh, right, yeah.'

'I thanked her for giving you that work, you know, clearing out her empty properties. Funny, I got the impression that she hadn't the foggiest what I was talking about.'

I fidgeted with my sleeves, avoiding eye contact. 'She's a bit ditzy, though, Mrs F.'

'Hmm. Homework done?'

I nodded.

He looked me up and down, his gaze resting on my new gear.

I shifted on my heels, uncomfortable.

'What's in the bag, Luke?'

I felt my face stiffen. 'Just school stuff.'

He wagged his finger. 'From now on, I'll be keeping a closer eye on you.'

Makes a change from the TV, I felt like saying. But I restrained myself.

The door slammed.

I caught my breath. I was skating on thin ice with the parents. I needed to be more careful. On the plus side, that was the longest conversation I'd had with Dad in months. It was a pleasant change from the usual grunts he emitted from the sitting-room chair. Maybe the ice caps at home were beginning to melt.

The curtains at the sitting room window twitched, and I spotted the shadow of Dad's face at the window. He tapped the glass and pointed his finger at me.

I turned and legged it.

$ $ $

'What time's he gonna be here?'

'Nine.' It was a quarter to nine now and nearly dark.

'What exactly did you say in the text?'

Finn smirked. 'That I was the Dark Bishop, and I wanted to talk to him about a possible business arrangement. Asked him to meet me at the top field in Conlons' farm.'

'And he actually bought that?'

Finn shrugged. 'He's desperate.'

I glanced over to where Koby was busy testing the drone. 'Ready, Kob?'

Koby gave us a thumbs-up.

'What's in the shopping bag?' said Finn.

'The lunchbox,' I whispered.

Finn's face dropped. 'You mean the beetle?'

'Dad was on a mission to hoover every room in the house. It couldn't stay under my bed.'

'Feck sake, Luke, a plastic bag – seriously? Stick it in my gear bag, quick.'

I unzipped the bag. 'Bloody hell, Finn. All the money's still in here.'

'I couldn't leave it at home, could I? Not with Mam on the warpath. She got wind of our little trip to the nail salon. Rita and her bloody big mouth. And it's not all the money – I gave Pablo a stash to mind.'

Finn clutched the lunchbox, squinting inside. 'How's he doing? Still alive in there?'

The beetle shuffled its body.

I groaned. 'Alive and kicking. Been keeping me awake with his ramming every night.'

We watched as Koby pushed the throttle on his remote control and the drone lifted off the ground.

'You know, we should drape something over the drone. Really put the frighteners on him,' Finn said, watching it hover nearby.

I made a face. 'Finn, it's a quadcopter. It needs the propellers to fly. You can't throw stuff over them.'

Finn thought for a minute. 'But we could put something around it, right? Like a coat?'

'Yeah, I guess.'

Finn put his finger on his chin. 'Who do we know with a long coat? I wonder …'

'Ha. I take it you're referring to that enormous overcoat that Koby rocked up in?' I figured it was another of Koby's lost-property scores. Even with all the money, he was still dipping into it.

'I'm surprised he can walk in it.'

'Just about.' I said. 'It trails along the ground like a cape.'

Finn scrambled to his feet. Within minutes, they had the overcoat taped securely to the underside of the drone. We manoeuvred ourselves into position. Koby, over the hedge with the drone. Finn, behind the tree, near the hedge. Me, lying in the long grass.

Finn rubbed his hands. 'Now, all we have to do is wait.'

'Not for long.' I gestured to a lone figure tramping over the hill.

'The eagle has landed,' Finn hissed through the hedge.

'HELLO,' shouted a voice.

'Yes,' Finn called out, in his deepest voice.

'Hello. Ach, is that the Dark Bishop?'

Finn swallowed a snigger. 'Y-yes.'

'It's Lochy. Lochy Mulgrew. I've come to have that wee chat.' He scoured the field nervously. 'Are ye gonna come out?'

'Can I trust you, Mulgrew, to keep my identity secret?'

'Aye, you can trust me. Ask anyone, I'm loyal to the bone.'

'Loyal,' Finn mouthed angrily, fist-pumping the air. He opened his mouth to react.

'Don't,' I said, afraid he'd lose it.

I whistled, our signal to Koby.

Within seconds, the drone was airborne, with the overcoat swaying in the breeze, brushing the tips of the grass as it moved. Koby expertly navigated it over the hedge, taking care not to catch the coat in the branches, and positioned it directly behind Lochy.

'I'm behind you,' said Finn.

Lochy spun on his heels.

'Aye, there you are.' Lochy nodded and marched up the field as if to introduce himself. The shadow glided towards him. Then Koby pushed the throttle, launching the drone up into the air.

Lochy's eyes engorged like golf balls. In a panic, he stumbled backwards onto the ground, scrambling around on his bum.

'He's spooked,' said Finn, pleased.

Then Koby switched on the LED lights, illuminating the top of the drone like a UFO.

Lochy shot up, shrieking like a baby. He tore down the hill, disappearing into the blackness below. After a minute, the shrieking stopped, the field eerily silent.

Then we heard a loud splash.

I hopped up. 'Where'd he go? Into the stream?'

Finn exploded with laughter. 'That was immense. Did you see his face? And the LEDs – top idea, Kob – that really knocked him into a cold sweat.'

Koby's head popped up over the hedge. 'Lads, you'd better go find him.'

'Ach, no need.'

Koby shone the drone light down the field. There stood Mulgrew, plucking sodden leaves from his hair, water dripping from every pore. 'You scabby muckers.'

'Ha, face it, Mulgrew. After that stunt with the betting book, leaving us dealing with TT Doherty, you deserve everything you get,' said Finn with a sneer. 'You knew your betting book was a sinking ship because of the payout you owed TT. But you still took our bank loan and got us involved in the shootout.'

Afterwards, watching Lochy attempt to dry himself with Koby's overcoat, I had a light-bulb moment. 'Lochy, don't you have a sister that works in the animal welfare place in town?'

'Aye, what about it?'

'We have a serious problem called Shay Doherty, TT's da,' I said. 'Your sister might just be able to help us get rid.'

'Shay? No way. On yer bike, Luke.' Lochy stepped back. 'I'm not holding hands with the Dohertys these days anyhow.'

I arched my eyebrow. Mulgrew was a piece of work. He was the reason we'd ended up in the clutches of TT Doherty in the first place. I gritted my teeth, trying to hold my temper. 'Aren't you forgetting something, Mulgrew? This is a camera drone. So everything that went on here tonight is on film.'

Finn laughed. 'It'd make entertaining online viewing, eh, Mulgrew?'

'The TV crew in school might even show an interest,' I added.

Lochy shrugged in surrender. Draining the water from his shoes, he slouched back in the direction of the farm.

$ $ $

'That was pure gold. Lochy got played. I told you it'd brighten up our day.' Finn noticed my face. 'What's up with you?'

I stared straight ahead. 'Finn, the gear bag, it's gone.'

'WHA'? No way.' Finn followed my gaze to an empty, flattened mound of grass.

I tried to speak, but no words formed in my head.

'It must be here. You must be lookin' in the wrong place, idiot,' Finn said dismissively, doing a full three-sixty to check the location. 'Sure, all these mounds of grass are the same.'

Finn swung up on the branch of a nearby tree and peered out over the field. 'Ha, see that big bulge in the hedge there? That's where Koby hid with the drone. We are miles off here.'

I pointed closer. 'Ground control to Finn. There's where Koby was with the drone.'

'No, you're way off target,' said Finn, swinging to the ground and racing off into the darkness to check.

I didn't budge.

I knew we were bang on. The bag had vaporised.

Eventually, Finn stalked back over, bag-less, and gripped my shoulder tight. 'Luke, snap out of it, man. The poxy bag, it's got to be here somewhere.'

I jerked my head slightly. 'I've looked all over.'

'Well, let's keep bloody looking.' Finn started slashing the long grass with his arms, panic setting in. 'Jaysus, it can't have just vanished. We didn't leave it long, only a few minutes.'

'Maybe Specks's da picked it up? Or one of the farm workers?' I said, grasping at straws.

'Cop on, Luke. What about Koby?'

'No, he headed home with the drone, never saw the bag.' I raised my voice to be heard over Finn's frantic grass thrashing. 'Finn, read my lips, somebody stole it.'

Finn ran his fingers through his hair. 'Luke. Look around – there's nobody here, for feck sake. It's just fields. And cows. Ah, don't tell me, you suspect the cows, right? You think the cows waddled over here and pinched it?'

I could feel the anger bubbling up inside. 'Yeah, that's it, Finn. Those pesky cows. Let's go over and negotiate with them to get our cash back. Maybe they'll be open to a deal, eh? Cos everybody and everything's for sale in your eyes.'

Finn collapsed against a tree, exhausted. 'Cheap shot. Nobody put a gun to your head to get involved.'

He was spot on. I was knee-deep in it too.

Finn banged the back of his head against the tree trunk repeatedly. 'Jaysus, all that cash. It couldn't get any worse.'

I bit my lip. 'And the beetle, Finn.'

Finn wailed loudly. 'Flippin' hell, the cash and the beetle. It's Armageddon.'

We sat in the dark for a while, contemplating our fate.

Finn clicked his fingers. 'Wait, what about Mulgrew?'

I shook my head vehemently. 'Ruled out. It's physically impossible. He was in front of us the whole time.' I glanced over at Finn cautiously. 'Should we expand the search? We're talkin' grade-A theft here.'

Finn bounced up, suddenly revved into action. 'Take out your phone. Let's get everyone we know up here. Anyone who owes us a favour. Pablo. Emily. Gabe. Speedy. Paddy. Mucker. The Tubbies. All of 'em. We need an army out searchin' for that gear bag.'

He marched down the field.

'C'mon. Let's find Specks. We need him on high alert.'

32

THE FILIPE BROTHERS

I spotted Koby's head straight away, behind a tower of books at the back of the library.

'Did you look at the accounts stuff I emailed?' I said awkwardly, joining him.

Koby made a face. 'There's a lot of money gone out. But nothing's coming in any more.'

The money train had derailed. With casualties. All the cash bundles under my mattress had evaporated with no replacements forthcoming.

I avoided eye contact. 'It's a botched job, Kob. Total hatchet. You got out at the right time.'

I yawned noisily, ignoring the filthy look from the nearby librarian. The hours spent combing the Conlons' farmland were taking their toll.

Koby scanned my face. 'The gear bag, still no sign?'

'Nada. We've had everyone out looking. Still nothing.' I pulled up my sleeves to reveal scrapes along both my arms. 'War wounds. From searching all those damn fields.'

Koby flinched. 'Nasty.'

'Listen, Kob, the drone camera, you're positive there's no clue on it?'

'Luke, I've scrutinised the footage. I didn't fly the drone over in the direction of the bag. You can take a look yourself, if you like.'

I sighed. Clutching at straws was becoming a habit.

Koby winced. 'So all the cash, it's gone?'

'Well, Finn gave an emergency stash to Pablo. We still have that.'

'This is an emergency.'

'We've moved into national-disaster territory.'

'Have you gone over the accounts with Emily? See if there's anywhere you could claw back some money?' Koby said.

I blushed, shifting uncomfortably. 'No, no, not yet.'

Koby threw me a sideways glance. 'Why, what's going on there?'

'Nothing,' I said.

'So speak to her. She might have an angle that we've missed.'

'Hmm, yeah,' I said, in my best non-committal tone.

Koby turned to face me and nudged my elbow. 'There *is* something going on. Spill.'

I gave in and described the awkward episode in the barn where we nearly locked lips.

'I've been avoiding her since, pretty much. Well, unless there are other people around,' I finished.

Koby sat back, grinning away at me. 'Actually, you two would make a good couple.'

'She's Finn's cousin, for starts.'

'So?'

'And then there's her and Pablo.'

'I thought that was all over.'

I squirmed. 'It is, but …'

'Ha, sounds like you've got it bad.'

'Shut up.'

Koby fished out his library card and went up to the desk with his mountain of books. I slumped back, picking up a discarded newspaper. I scanned the front-page stories. A headline about a hotel closing in town. Another about a herd of cattle destroying a championship golf course. A scandal about a politician.

Then I spotted a story in the corner: 'Brothers wanted after spate of robberies.'

> Two Brazilian brothers, aged eighteen, are wanted for questioning in connection with a spate of cash robberies. The men are posing as tourists and travelling up the coast.

I stared at the two faces in the grainy black-and-white photo. Why did they look familiar? I reread the article. Brazilian brothers. Brazilian brothers. Then it clicked: the hipsters that turned up to camp at the Conlons' place. Spate of cash robberies.

I grabbed my phone. 'Finn, I know where our gear bag is.'

$ $ $

'You gave Specks a hundred-euro loan for that?'

Finn stood back. 'You gotta admit, it's one hell of a disco ball.'

I stared at the shimmering silver globe hanging majestically in the centre of the barn. My mind wandered back to our first meeting in the butcher's shop. Koby and his Post-its. We did exactly what we said we wouldn't do: we lost control. And now we owed TT Doherty a lot of money. Money that we didn't have. Correction: money that the FFP Bank didn't have. I wasn't clawing into my savings for anyone, even a snake like Doherty.

And there was the not-so-small matter of the missing beetle.

'C'mon,' said Finn, shoving me. 'Before they do a vanishing act.'

We met Specks at the entrance to the campsite, complete with torch and walkie-talkie. We followed him in silence until we reached the two lone coffin tents, pitched in the middle of a soggy field.

Specks approached the tents, shouting. 'Filipes. Get out here.'

After a moment, some evidence of life emerged, as darts of light from a phone screen shone through the canvas. At the nearest tent, Filipe One's head appeared, rubbing his eyes.

Specks flashed his torch. 'OUT, now. Before I call the cops.'

Filipe One blinked rapidly. 'What … what's happening?'

Specks stepped closer. 'OUT.' He held up the walkie-talkie. 'I've Da on the other end of this, if there's any trouble.'

After frantic unzipping and urgent whispers, the Filipes finally wriggled out in their sleeping bags, still half-comatose.

'Where's our bag, punk?' Finn said, surging forward.

'I no understand,' Filipe One stuttered.

Specks caught Finn's arm. 'Waste of time. They don't speak a word.'

'They know more than they're letting on,' I said warily.

'Go in and look for it,' Specks said, pointing to the open tents. 'I'll keep an eye on these bucks. They're half-asleep anyway.'

Finn hurdled over Filipe One and nose-dived into one tent, while I sidestepped a dozy-looking Filipe Two and tackled the second one. I emptied the huge rucksack. Nothing, except clothes that hadn't seen a washing machine in a while.

'Anything, Finn?'

'Not unless you count a rock-hard pizza slice and some mouldy fruit.'

'Wait.' I spotted the corner of a lunchbox peeking out from underneath the tent cover. 'Where'd you get this?'

Filipe One's eyes flickered. 'We found. In camping kitchen.'

'Right, where's the beetle?' I removed the lid, turning the lunchbox upside down and pointing inside. 'The bee-tle.'

No response.

I glanced over just in time to catch the brothers exchange a knowing look. Right then, I knew we were being played.

I decided to switch tactics.

'You know David Romero?'

The brothers' necks popped up like chickens.

'Man-ches-ter City,' said Filipe Two, eyes shining.

I whipped out the Golden Tickets, still nestling in my pocket since our nail-salon escapade. I held a ticket out for them to read.

'Very profitable. You can sell for lots of money,' I said, like I was speaking to toddlers. 'You give us the beetle. And we give you these tickets.'

Filipe One cocked his head. He pulled off his baggie beanie hat and rustled inside, producing a matchbox. He slid the matchbox open, just enough for me to see the tiny horns.

I flung the envelope on the ground.

Filipe One tossed the matchbox at my feet.

'Is it alive?' said Finn, darting over.

I nudged the beetle. Its legs flickered. 'Just about.'

'Feck sake, if TT Doherty saw his precious beetle in a matchbox, face it, we'd all be dead men walking,' Finn murmured.

Carefully, I tipped the beetle into the lunchbox, chucking

in a few small pieces of rotten apple. 'Sorry, bud, better than nothing.'

'At least we have something to give to TT now,' Finn said glumly. 'No sign of the cash. These donkeys don't seem to have a clue.'

'They're cleverer than they look, Finn.'

My eyes flickered back to the brothers, gushing over the tickets, still squirming around in the sleeping bags like giant worms.

I hit my forehead. 'Duh, Finn, we're so stupid.'

'What?'

'C'mon, it's so obvious.'

I dropped the lunchbox and dashed over, catching Filipe One by surprise, and pinned his arms from behind. 'Get him out of the sleeping bag, Finn.'

Finn gripped the end of the bag, but Filipe One resisted hard, kicking and tussling. 'Hold him down, Luke.'

'I'm trying.'

Specks bolted over and belly-flopped onto Filipe One's chest.

Finn wrestled the sleeping bag away.

'Open it,' I said, releasing my grip on Filipe One.

Finn unzipped it quickly. At the bottom, all warm from being at Filipe's feet, lay a snug bundle of multi-coloured socks, stuffed full of cash.

'Bingo,' yelled Finn triumphantly.

I pointed across the field. 'Damn, the other one's bolted.' Undetected, Filipe Two had crawled out and legged it, sleeping bag in hand, in the direction of the farm.

Specks reached for the walkie-talkie. 'Specks to Base. Specks to Base.'

'Base here.'

'Da, catch hold o' that fella' running towards the house. Copy that.'

'Roger.'

'Don't worry – Da'll see to him,' Specks said confidently.

I put my finger to my lips. 'What's that humming noise? D'you hear it?'

'An engine,' Specks said, pointing to the main road. 'It's coming from over there.'

Suddenly, we were blinded by headlights. A quad bike blasted its way over the hill, wheels spinning in the air. It came to a blistering halt, skidding across the ground, spraying muck in every direction.

TT Doherty leapt off the quad.

'Ah-ha. I've been lookin' for you boys all over. And you've got my cash all ready for me. Nice,' he said, pointing at Finn, who was still shifting rolls of money from the socks.

He headed straight for the money, but stopped. 'Hold it.' He pointed, voice quivering. 'Is that my beetle?'

I followed his glare to where the lunchbox was thrown on the grass amongst the pizza box and rotten fruit.

Abandoned.

Like a piece of rubbish.

I gulped, anticipating the fallout.

TT almost tripped over himself to reach it. He lifted the lid and peeked inside. His face contorted like he'd stuck his finger into a live socket.

'This guy stole your beetle and kept him in a matchbox,' I blurted, pointing to Filipe One. 'They nearly suffocated him.'

TT's head darted from me to Filipe One. Trying to decide who to obliterate first, I figured.

Thankfully, he made a run for Filipe.

At that moment, we were encircled by a sea of flashing lights.

'What on earth is going on here?'

A guard appeared at the campsite entrance.

Then a second.

Then two more.

One shone a torch on the TT-and-Filipe-One scuffle.

Another on the mountain of socks.

Another on our white faces.

'Well, well. We've had a complaint from the neighbours about a disturbance, but it looks like there's more to it, eh. You two, over there, get up.'

Grudgingly, TT released a battered-looking Filipe One.

Recognition flickered on the guard's face. 'Ah, young Doherty. What a surprise. You, where do you think you're going?'

Two guards immediately sprang from the blackness and grasped Filipe One, who'd started slowly slinking down the hill.

'Who owns this?' The spotlight fell on the mountain of socks overflowing with banknotes.

Nobody said a word.

The guard gritted his teeth. 'Maybe you didn't quite hear me. I said, who owns this? I'll take everybody down to the station unless you start talking.'

This time, we all spoke at once.

'They do,' said Filipe One, pointing at us.

'Him,' I replied, pointing at TT.

'Them,' said TT, jabbing his finger at us.

'Him,' Finn said, gesturing towards TT.

The guard exhaled noisily. He marched over and flipped the socks with his foot. 'OK, who owns the socks?'

We all pointed at Filipe One.

I made eye contact with Finn. The money was pretty much lost to us now. The police would see to that. Time to pull the plug on the Brazilians. Otherwise we'd all be banged up.

Finn read my thoughts exactly. 'That Brazilian lad's wanted for cash robberies in other towns. It was in the paper. Him and his brother.'

'My da's got the brother up at the house,' Specks added. 'He tried to do a runner.'

The guard scrutinised Filipe One closely. 'Round them up,' he ordered.

Within minutes, they had the Filipe brothers in a patrol car and had confiscated our money. They decided to drag TT back for questioning too. Probably because he was a Doherty. And they discovered he'd no legal documentation to drive the quad.

Amongst this turbulence, we tried to discreetly make our escape.

A guard stood in our way. 'Not so fast. Where do you boys fit into this picture?'

'Oh, they just stopped by to see our barn. It's the venue for our school disco, you see. We came down here to investigate when we heard all the noise,' Specks piped up, winking at us behind the guard's back.

'Bit late for social visits, isn't it? Especially at your age?'

Cue innocent faces, complete with bottom-lip pouts.

'Go on, my colleague will drop you into the village. And stay out of trouble. Remember, I've got your details.'

$ $ $

We walked home the long way after the guards dropped us off.

'Close call,' I said, breaking the silence.

'Too close.'

'D'you think the guards will ring our parents?'

But Finn's mind was elsewhere. 'We can kiss goodbye to all that cash. There's no way we'll get it back now.'

I pictured the guards arriving at our door.

And Mam and Dad's faces. It wouldn't be pretty.

'Just thinkin', Mucker Burke won't be impressed. We've just given away his Golden Tickets,' Finn said, stopping at the corner of his road.

I looked up. 'I take it you didn't see the footie highlights at the weekend?'

'No, why?'

'David Romero. He's pulled his hamstring. Meant to be in a bad way. Can't play. But, more importantly, can't travel.'

Finn stood still. 'So, the event –'

I smiled. 'Cancelled.'

Finn's mouth dropped. 'You knew the tickets were worthless all along.'

I said nothing.

'Clever play, Lukey, clever play.'

'And we've still got one bargaining chip left.' I tapped the lunchbox with the beetle curled up snugly inside.

Finn turned up the street. 'And our emergency stash with Pablo. Not so bad.'

33

BIG BEN

Finn covered his face and gazed out through the gaps in his fingers. 'What do you think?'

I made a face. 'Painful.'

Finn nodded.

'Why isn't he moving around?' I asked.

'Dunno. He looks constipated.'

We were standing at the back of the hall watching the final rehearsal for the school musical. Pablo was on stage practising one of his key scenes.

Miss Shine walked by and stopped in front of Finn, stony-faced. 'You sold me a dud, Mr Fitzpatrick.'

Finn frowned. 'Miss?'

'Can't you see for yourself?' She threw up her arm in the direction of the stage, where Pablo was tiptoeing across like a jittery crab. It was cringeworthy.

'Mr Silva suffers from stage-fright,' she continued. 'Frankly, I've never seen a less artful-looking Artful Dodger.'

Miss Shine stalked off.

I watched as she barked at some poor innocent in her path. 'She's not happy.'

Finn shrugged. 'We've bigger problems.'

Pablo appeared. 'Guys, how do I look up there?'

'Awful,' said Finn.

Pablo laughed unashamedly. 'Ha, I know. I am terrible.'

At least he didn't seem all that bothered. The wad of money that Finn had bribed him with probably helped ease the pain.

'Watch out for Mizz Shine. She isn't a happy lady,' Pablo advised.

'We've already had the pleasure,' I said.

'Pablo, this isn't a social visit,' said Finn suddenly. 'We've been tryin' to get hold of you. That emergency stash I gave you. I need it back, like, super-super-urgently.'

Pablo cocked his head to the side. 'You told me to put it in a really safe place.'

'Yeah, but I need it back now. Today. Seeing as the rest of our money's gone walk-about.'

Pablo scrunched up his nose. 'Put it somewhere that nobody would be able to find it, you said.'

Finn sighed loudly. 'Yes, yes, I know I said that, but I need it.'

'Where's the money, Pablo?' I said, sensing that this could go on forever.

'I hid it in a really great place.'

'Which is?' I prompted.

Pablo raised his eyes up to the ceiling.

We followed his gaze.

'Bloody hell.'

'What on earth is that?'

Hanging from the roof: a huge construction made entirely from papier mâché.

'Hey, it's Big Ben,' Pablo said, as if it were obvious. 'You know, the clock.'

'What's it for?' I said, wondering how we didn't notice this mass structure hovering overhead before.

'It's a prop for the musical. For the London street scenes.'

Finn pointed up to the roof. 'But what's that got to do with –?' He stopped speaking. 'Feck sake, please tell me you didn't put our emergency stash up there?'

Pablo pouted.

I bit my lip.

Finn glared at me. 'It's not funny, Luke.'

I swallowed a laugh. 'I know, I know.'

'Not when we haven't a penny to give to TT Doherty.'

'Talk about a string of disasters, though.' It felt like we were part of a bad comedy skit.

Finn turned to Pablo. 'How did you get it in there? The money?'

'The day you gave me the bag of notes, well, that was the same day that they were practising the clock movements, up and down.'

A group of first-years walked by. Finn put his hand out to signal to Pablo to lower his voice. We moved over to the side of the hall.

'Go on.'

Pablo leaned against the wall, yawning. 'I spotted a small gap at the back of the clock. So, I thought, per-fect. Nobody will find it in there. I threw the money in and it rolled right into the middle, out of sight.'

Finn chewed over this information but said nothing. Pablo rubbed his eyes fiercely. The back-to-back rehearsals were obviously taking their toll. Miss Shine enjoyed cracking the whip.

'How did you plan to get the bag back out?' I said eventually.

Pablo shrugged. 'Easy. Once the show is over, the clock is going into storage in the art room.'

We all gazed up.

'We're mincemeat,' Finn proclaimed. 'We'll never get the money outta that yoke before TT Doherty's deadline.'

'When's the deadline?' Pablo asked.

'Friday,' I replied. 'Sports day.'

Pablo clenched his jaw. 'It's tight, man. The show opens tomorrow night.'

Something niggled in my brain. 'Wait, didn't you say that the clock is lowered during the show?'

'Yes.'

'So, can't we just lower it down now when this place clears?'

'It's complicated to move. The engineering class designed and constructed the controls.'

'So who's in charge of it then? Who lowers the clock during the show?' I said.

Finn twigged. 'Exactly. Who do we have to pay off to get that clock down?'

Pablo shuddered. 'Trust me, you don't want to go there, man.'

'Who is it?'

Pablo hesitated. 'Kimberley Farrell.'

I turned to Finn. 'Great. Your number one fan.'

Finn slapped his forehead. 'Kim "Chip on My Shoulder" Farrell.'

'We have to persuade her to move the clock before the show tomorrow night,' I said.

'Well, she's not going to speak to me,' Finn said, stating the obvious. 'I'm still "Public Enemy Number One" as far as she's concerned. Drama queen.'

Classic memory lapse from Finn.

'You did break it off with her over loudspeaker on cup-final day.'

'That was years ago. Get over it.'

'She's not a huge fan of mine either,' I said, primarily due to my association with Finn. I gestured at Pablo. 'You'll have to do it.'

Finn clicked his fingers. 'Perfect. Kimberley will fall for your Argentinian charms.'

Pablo hesitated. 'I'm not so sure. She called me a "tone-deaf, airbrushed gringo" yesterday.'

'She's no pushover,' I agreed.

'Lads, I'm afraid she's our only option.'

34

KIM 'CHIP ON MY SHOULDER'

'No way.'

'Please, Kimberley.'

'For starters, remove him from here.' She pointed at Finn.

Finn didn't budge.

I glared at him.

'OK, OK, I'll just stand over here.' Finn took a few hasty steps backwards.

'Kimberley, pleeease, I need your help,' Pablo said.

Kimberley scanned her eyes over the lighting control switchboard, totally ignoring him.

Pablo smiled lazily at her and touched her arm briefly. 'Kimberley. Kim.' His brown eyes widened as he gazed at her. It was the full-blown Pablo treatment. Normally it worked a treat. 'I left my phone down in the hall earlier, and one of the lads picked it up and threw it into the clock. A practical joke.'

'And?' said Kim in a low growl.

'You know I suffer from stage-fright,' said Pablo. 'The phone has my special tunes to help me relax before the performance. Mizz Shine likes me to listen to my relaxation music.'

I stepped in closer and put a hand on Pablo's shoulder. 'It's true. Inside, he's a ball of nerves.'

'Oh, really?' said Kimberley sceptically. 'That's such a shame.'

Pablo threw Kimberley his famed puppy-dog eyes.

'The show must go on,' I threw in, cringing.

Kimberley flicked a switch. 'Not my problem. Get yourself a self-help book.'

'But my phone might ring in the middle of the performance,' Pablo said, trying another tack and still smiling despite the frostiness. 'It's on full volume.'

'Boo hoo. We'll know who ruined the show if it rings.'

'Please, Kimberley,' Pablo said, with more than a hint of desperation.

Kimberly scowled at him, then glanced at her watch. 'Out. The show is going to kick off soon. I'm not lowering the clock for you morons.'

'It'd only take a minute or two,' Finn piped up. 'C'mon, Kim, for old times.'

Kimberley froze.

Instantly, the atmosphere in the room nose-dived to sub-zero.

I turned around. Big mistake, Finn. Mammoth.

'You and me don't have any old times, Fitzpatrick. I've erased all that from my memory. I've deleted you completely from my life. You no longer exist in my world, get it?'

Whoa. Turns out, that chip on her shoulder was boulder-like.

'All right, chill, Kim. It's been over two years.'

Deathly silence.

'Don't you think you're over-reacting a tad?' Finn said, mistaking the silence for an invitation to keep digging himself into a pit. 'We've all moved on, right?'

He'd already taken things a step too far. Now he was on a path of self-destruction.

I raised my hand. 'Finn, enough.'

It was game over.

Kim stood up, pale-faced. 'You made a total fool out of me, Fitzpatrick. Now you come crawlin' back here lookin' for a favour. Not a chance.'

The sound of a microphone testing could be heard from the stage.

'Now get out, all of you,' she hissed. 'OUT before I –'

BOOM.

A loud blast reverberated around the hall, echoing up into the lighting box.

'What the –?' Kimberley raced over and snapped open the hatch on the wall to reveal the drama in the hall below.

'BUCKET SCAM. BUCKET SCAM.'

'WE WANT OUR MONEY. WE WANT OUR MONEY.'

'BATTERED DEAL.'

I bolted towards the hatch, crawling over the equipment, and squeezed my head through.

Mona Lisa Murphy stood on the edge of the stage like the head cheerleader, spinning the microphone wire like a baton. In the hall, people were standing on chairs, drumming on empty buckets and chanting angrily. They held up 'Wanted' posters with Gabe's grainy mugshot plastered underneath. Looking more frenzied than usual, Gabe's photo was like something from the FBI's Most Wanted list.

'What is happening?' said Pablo, cocking his ear. 'That song, it's not in the show.'

'It's not a song. It's a flippin' protest,' I said, catching Finn's eye.

Mona Lisa's voice bounced off the walls: 'GIVE US WHAT WE WERE PROMISED.'

The crowd erupted.

'A mass rally, more like.' Finn nudged in beside me, eyes widening. 'That Murphy's a crowd-pleaser.'

I watched as Mona Lisa stamped her foot and punched the air to the beat of the chant. 'I told you she was dangerous.'

'Still, at least Gabe's pickin' up the slack,' said Finn, nodding at the posters.

I pointed out the hatch. 'Eh, I wouldn't be so sure of that.'

Right at that moment, Mona Lisa Murphy swept up a gigantic placard with Finn's grinning face transposed onto an image of the *Star Wars* gangster Jabba the Hutt.

Underneath, the words: 'Finn Fitzpatrick – this piece of slime has stolen our money!'

The crowd went wild.

Then another poster – this time, a naff holiday selfie, with the word 'Common Crook' scrawled across it.

'Ugh.' Finn gasped loudly, shielding his eyes. 'Why'd they use that pic?'

With his aviator shades and gold chain, Finn looked like a Z-list celebrity. 'Erm, lovin' those shades. Let me guess, your week in Barcelona?'

Finn missed the sarcasm in my voice, nodding proudly. 'Yeah. I totally rocked the smooth bronzed-chest look that summer.'

I didn't respond, instead turning my attention to Mona Lisa's crew gathering below us.

'Not sure about the whiter-than-white teeth,' Finn continued, grimacing.

'Eh, focus.' Finn was more concerned with his Hollywood teeth than the fact that he was top of the school hit list.

'Looks like you're quite the crowd-pleaser yourself, Fitzpatrick,' drawled a soft voice from behind.

We swung around.

Kimberley.

I'd almost forgotten she was there.

Kimberley sat deep into her chair, observing Finn closely, a large, self-satisfied grin spreading across her face. 'Well, well, well. Let's see if I have this right. There's a horde of angry rioters down there all lookin' for you ... all spillin' for your guts. And here yooou are –'

I gulped, sensing what was coming.

Kimberley placed her headset on her head, tugging the mic close to her mouth, and pointed to the hatch. 'Fitzpatrick, this microphone is connected to the speakers on stage. What's to stop me telling that mob exactly where you are?'

We were cornered.

Finn stared at her, mouth zipped shut. It was unusual for him to be lost for words.

Right on cue, the noise from the hall got louder.

Kimberley cupped her ear, smiling sweetly. 'Oh dear. They do sound quite vicious. Like they really mean business.'

Finally reality kicked in and Finn jumped into action. He plastered on his most convincing Prince Charming face. 'Kim. Babe.'

Kimberly stiffened.

Finn put out his hands. 'You're totally bluffing. I know you wouldn't hang me.'

'Wanna bet?'

Finn moved closer, ignoring Kimberley's over-the-top flinching. 'You're too nice. And you're not a snitch, Kim. Unlike me, you actually have some morals.'

Kimberley growled, banging the desk. 'Same cocky, vain, selfish, smarmy Finn Fitzpatrick. You haven't changed a bit.'

In the corner, Pablo swallowed a giggle. 'Harsh, man.'

I gazed from Finn to Kimberley and back again, debating whether to intervene. Half of me wanted to see how this showdown panned out on its own. Finn had created a monster.

Then Kimberley went to flick on the microphone switch.

That decided it.

I was in.

I slammed my hand on the desk, blocking her. 'Look, Kim, I'm sure there's something we can do to sort this all out.'

'You can't buy me off,' said Kimberley.

I stood firm. 'There must be something. Finn's up for anything, right, Finn?'

'Eh, right, sound,' said Finn reluctantly.

Kimberley swung around on her chair, facing Finn. 'All right, there is something. An apology. I want an apology for the pathetic, low-life way you treated me.'

Finn almost choked. 'A what?'

I dropped my head in my hands. That was that. Ceasefire talks suspended. Getting blood from a stone would be easier.

A thunder-clap echoed up from the hall.

I poked my head out the hatch.

I could see bulging biceps bounding to the stage.

The rugby team.

The forwards swooped Mona Lisa Murphy up like a feather, placed her in a king's chair and paraded her around the stage, joining the chant.

'WE WANT OUR MONEY. WE WANT OUR MONEY.'

Kimberley peeked over my shoulder, enjoying every minute. 'Jeez, is that the rugby team joining the party? You've upset them too? Bad move.'

I turned to Finn, hoping the voracious roars would spur him into action.

Finn froze, like he was staring down the barrel of a gun.

I prodded him. 'Finn?'

No reaction.

I dragged Finn by the jumper, resisting the urge to shake him hard. 'Finn, cop on. We've been ambushed. And she looks ready to feed us to the wolves.'

Pablo ran over to back up my efforts. 'Finn man, just apologise. You need to gobble your ego.'

I eyebrowed Pablo. 'Swallow your pride?'

Pablo's face lit up. 'Swallow your pride, exactly, exactly.'

'I'm waiting,' Kimberley sang, her finger hovering over the switch.

I banged my foot on the floor. 'Finn, listen to that noise. It's carnage down there.'

Finn punched the air, biting down hard on his lower lip.

'Do it,' I said, more forcefully than I meant to.

Finn leaned against my shoulder. 'All right, all right, steady. I'll do it.'

I closed my eyes, relieved.

'I apologise,' Finn muttered, basically to the wall.

'Ahem,' said Kimberley, legs crossed, unimpressed.

'Jaysus, Finn.' I grabbed hold of his shoulders and edged him around to face Kimberley head on. 'Again.'

'OK, I apologise. Happy?' said Finn, eyes flashing.

Kimberley rolled her eyes. 'Yeah, like that was sooo sincere.'

The floor shuddered as the protest stepped up a gear.

Finn relented, meeting her icy stare, shoulders stooped. 'Look, Kim. I'm sorry. It was a poxy thing to do.'

'Poxy. Poxy. Eh, that's quite an understatement. What about shocking?'

Finn half-nodded.

'Horrendous?'

She took a step closer to Finn.

'Repulsive?'

Another step.

'Vile? I could go on.'

Please don't, I prayed silently. Even though Kimberley's rant was buying us valuable time, I could see Finn's patience was fading fast.

Kimberley waved her finger in Finn's face. 'And I want the apology over loudspeaker on sports day. Where everybody can hear,' she said, seizing the opportunity to deal a final humiliating blow. 'So you know what it feels like.'

She was milking it. But, seriously, who could blame her?

Finn shoved his hands deep into his pockets.

Kimberley took his silence as victory and clasped her hands together, drowning in her own smugness. 'Ah, revenge is most definitely sweet.'

This love-in was interrupted by the unmistakeable sound of a headache-inducing screech from below: Miss Shine.

She'd discovered the protest.

After five to six screeches, the hall was clear.

I threw Finn a look.

We'd got away with it.

The protesters had moved on. For now.

But we were on a slippery slope.

'Two minutes,' Finn called out as we walked back down the stairs.

'Huh?'

'If Shiner had been two minutes earlier I'd have got away with promising that flippin' apology.'

35

CONFETTI CARNAGE

'That went well.'

Finn glanced back up towards the lighting box, rolling his eyes. 'She's highly strung, Kimberley Farrell, always was.'

Finn still didn't get it. You couldn't trample all over people and get away with it. Sooner or later it catches up with you.

Pablo creased up his face, looking distraught. 'Hmm.'

Finn lobbed him a friendly punch. 'What's wrong with you? You weren't the one humiliated up there.'

I copped it. 'He's in shock. For once, his legendary charm tactics didn't work.'

Finn laughed. 'Even the puppy-dog eyes were a fail.'

Pablo seemed genuinely perplexed. 'Hey, man, it's never happened before.'

Finn placed his hand on Pablo's shoulder. 'You're losin' it, amigo.'

'What? No. It must be this crazy outfit,' said Pablo, pulling at the tattered rags that made up his Victorian costume.

'That waistcoat isn't a great look,' said Finn.

I sniffed. 'There's a serious whiff off it too. It honks.'

Finn pulled us into a group huddle. 'What are we gonna do, lads? Not only have we got TT Doherty squeezin' us for our last few euro, now we have Mona Lisa Murphy and her squad of protein pushers after us too. Face it, we're still no closer to gettin' our hands on that clock.'

'Not necessarily,' I said, taking out my phone.

Finn looked over my shoulder. 'What you got?'

'A photo I took upstairs. It lists the times that Kim lowers the clock during the show. The sheet was on the desk.'

'Champion.' Finn thought for a moment. 'What're we gonna do with it, though?'

I pointed to the first time on the sheet: 20.20. 'Well, somebody will have to sneak backstage and try to grab the money when the clock is down during the show.'

Pablo and I looked straight at Finn.

'What? Me?'

'You messed up our chances with Kimberley,' I said. 'Time to pay up.'

Finn puffed out his cheeks. 'Fine. How'll we do this?'

I pointed to the side of the stage. 'You need to go hover inconspicuously around that ladder.'

'Mr Silva, there you are.'

We all jumped.

Miss Shine stalked over and shoved a black bowler hat into Pablo's hands. 'You're needed in make-up immediately. Curtain-up in eight minutes.'

Pablo disappeared.

Miss Shine frowned. 'And you two, what are you even doing up here? Scram.'

We veered away towards the exit, but once we were out of Miss Shine's line of vision, Finn scarpered towards the ladder.

I headed to the back of the hall to watch from a distance. Beside me the TV documentary team were setting up their equipment, presumably to film the much-anticipated opening performance. I hoped somebody had warned them to bring some earplugs.

After a long eight minutes, the curtain came up.

I watched the opening scene unfold, keeping an eye on the time.

20.15.

Pablo appeared on stage, his singing bursts marginally improved since rehearsals, probably helped by the addition of the school choir, who were squeezed in under the stage.

20.19.

20.20.

The curtain fell to prepare for the scene change.

My stomach flipped. I looked up and spotted the large clock face slowly edging down behind the veiled material.

The curtain shot up, revealing a backdrop of a London street in Victorian times, complete with Big Ben hovering in the background.

As the show progressed, I could see the clock rocking back and forth, gently at first, but gaining momentum. I guessed that Finn was doing his best to reach the money.

In between the actors' lines, I heard a bang, followed by urgent whispers. I spotted shadows darting behind the stage backdrop. Then the clock fell slightly, almost slipping off its rails. The structure spun around, shifting the clock face towards the ceiling, with the back of the clock towards the floor.

I glanced up at the lighting box.

The hatch burst open and an anxious-looking Kimberley peered out.

The clock began to move again, slowly at first, edging out towards the audience, but it quickly gained speed. As the actors became distracted by the clock in motion, I realised that this evidently wasn't part of the script. The performance had virtually come to a standstill.

This had Finn written all over it.

Once the clock reached the centre of the hall, it jerked slightly, and the back burst open. A mass of colourful, sparkly confetti spurted out. And with it, our bag of money. Confetti and banknotes floated down like snow onto the bemused audience.

Miss Shine rushed on stage like a mini tornado, yelling up at the lighting box. Meanwhile, beside me, the TV crew were rubbing their hands gleefully, as the entire fiasco was captured on film.

Suddenly Finn appeared by my side. 'Hmm, didn't go exactly to plan.'

'What happened?'

'I couldn't get a hand to the bag. Then I fell off the ladder and knocked the clock forward.'

I groaned. 'You must have knocked it onto the wrong rail. Did anyone spot you?'

'Hard to know.'

I gazed at the spray of sparkling confetti and banknotes. 'This must have been for the grand finale.'

Some of the audience scrambled from their seats, jostling and elbowing to grab the money.

Finn stared at the chaotic scene unfolding. He put his hand

out and caught a piece of confetti. 'This could be *our* grand finale. Look at our bloody emergency stash, all over the hall floor. No, no way, I'm not havin' it.'

With that, Finn dived onto the floor, arms outstretched like an eagle's wings, hoovering up money as he slid up the centre aisle on his stomach. I joined in, clambering around the first few seats of each row, desperately grabbing notes and confetti from between people's feet, apologising as I went, and stuffing it all down the front of my jacket.

As I got nearer the front, I spotted Miss Shine and Powder in a huddle. Miss Shine's head shot up, and she pointed straight at us.

I pulled Finn's arm and dragged him to his feet. 'C'mon, I think we've been burnt.'

Finn made a final grab for a five-euro note that had dropped at his foot. Then he followed me out the side door.

Exit stage left.

$ $ $

There was a loud knock on my bedroom door. Mam barged in, face boiling, coat still on after her late shift.

'Luke, I got a call during work.'

My stomach heaved. Oh no. This was it. The guards.

'From the school.'

I stuffed my face into the pillow, hiding my relief.

'Something to do with disrupting the school play. The principal says you're on a final warning – next time, suspension. So you can consider yourself grounded, indefinitely. No going anywhere without permission.'

I didn't bother arguing.

'Count yourself lucky your father's not here,' she muttered.

I poked my head out from under the duvet. 'He's not?'

'No, he's out.'

'That makes a change.'

She turned and looked straight at me. 'Luke, I know things haven't been easy. But we got a buyer for the business this week. The offer wasn't as much as your dad had hoped. But it's enough to keep us going here until he finds work. And he got a lead on a job this evening.'

I nodded back at her. Things might get back to normal now.

'Oh, I almost forgot, I was talking to Finn's mother. She's only delighted with your offer to help with her empty properties. Be at her office tomorrow morning at eight.'

I shot up. 'But it's the weekend.'

'So?'

'My only lie-in.'

'Tough.'

I lay back down.

'Mam?'

'Yeah.'

I peered out. 'So, no more soup?'

Mam bit her lip, trying not to smile. 'No, no more psychedelic soup.'

36

THE APOLOGY

Finn rolled the last five-euro note into a neat ball, held it between his thumb and forefinger and lined up the brown paper bag in the middle of the table.

I pulled at the bag handle. Inside was a mound of tattered, trodden, scrunched-up five- and ten-euro balls, intermixed with tiny shards of sparkly confetti. There was a strong whiff of bacon too. Probably related to the jumbo breakfast roll that Gabe had just demolished.

I stared at Finn. 'How much?'

He leaned back and threw the final fiver neatly into the bag. 'Slam dunk.'

I tried Emily instead. 'How much?'

Emily blinked. 'Enough. Just.'

I nodded and flicked the bag in Gabe's general direction.

Finn swiped the table. 'Start with the rugby team, Gabe. No question. We need to get those mush boys off our backs.'

We all nodded simultaneously.

'Then the soccer lads,' said Finn, probably imagining the frosty atmosphere in the dressing room next year.

I glanced over to where Gabe was ceremoniously lifting the

café table up with one hand. The bag of cash slid towards him, which he whipped up, delighted.

'No, pay the hurling team back next. I mean, c'mon, Finn, we're talkin' fifteen Gabe's – with big sticks.'

Finn observed Gabe for a millisecond. 'Hurling gets my vote.'

Gabe popped up. 'Hockey?'

Finn slapped Gabe on the back. 'Girls' hockey team. Nah, last on the list, bro.'

In the corner, Emily clucked loudly.

Finn put up his hand. 'Don't go there, Em. Don't go there with all that girl-power pants. Not now.'

'So soccer, then basketball?' I said hurriedly, thinking of the six-footers that had surrounded me in the corridor. 'And if there's anything left over – tennis team?'

Finn snorted. 'Tennis. Seriously, Luke? I'd rather keep the leftovers.'

'Wait, what about the cardio bunnies? Are they sorted?' Last thing we needed was any confrontation with the gang of fanatical bodybuilders from our year.

'Tennis is out. The gym heroes are in,' said Finn.

I thought back to the protest in the hall. And its ringleader. 'Finn, you definitely took care of Mona Lisa Murphy? She won't come back to bite us?'

'Sorted. She got all her savings back. With sprinkles on top.' Finn glanced at his watch. 'Gabe, get on your bike, mate. I need everyone paid off by the morning.'

'Tomorrow morning?' said Emily, surprised.

I narrowed my eyes, wondering what the sudden urgency was. Considering Finn had slobbered over the cash for the guts of a week, meaning we'd had to creep around the school like fugitives, trying to avoid Mona Lisa Murphy and her band of militants.

Finn flung Gabe his coat, pointing him towards the café door. 'Beat it, bozo.'

'Finn. Spill, what's the story?' I said, spotting him squirm ever so slightly.

'All right, all right. It's Mona Lisa Murphy –'

'Feck sake. What now? I thought you said she was sorted?'

Finn sighed loudly. 'She's lined up the reality-TV crew for tomorrow. Plans to nail us in a tell-all interview unless we pay everyone back. We'd be on Powder's hit list for "like, eternity". Her words.'

I gritted my teeth. I should've guessed that there was more to Finn's declaration to 'do the right thing' and his sudden desire to pay all the savers back with the cash that we'd scraped off the hall floor.

We needed to stay under Powder's radar for a while, though. We'd just about got away with the school-musical circus. Despite a lengthy investigation, Powder had only managed to put us at the scene of the crime. So far. But he was waiting in the long grass.

We'd no choice but to meet Mona Lisa's deadline.

I shoved Gabe off his seat. 'Move it, big man.'

'What about TT?' I said, when Gabe had finally left – though not before ordering two egg rolls for his journey. 'We're completely bankrupt.'

'Ha, a bankrupt bank, pathetic,' said Finn, a slow smile forming on his face. Then he looked me straight in the eye. 'Y'know, TT Doherty can take a running jump. We'll reunite him with the love of his life, that dumb insect, and that's his lot as far as I'm concerned.'

That'd go down like a lead balloon. 'I'll let you break that news to him, Finn.'

$ $ $

'Here he is. Robin Hood on two wheels.' I pointed to a lone hooded figure, peddling like crazy across the school pitch with a total disregard for the various sports-day events taking place.

Finn rolled his eyes. 'Finally.'

I cringed as Gabe bolted straight through the middle of the athletics track, shielding my eyes. 'Ohh. He nearly flattened a couple of sprinters there.'

Finn squinted. 'What's he doin' now?'

Gabe circled the outside track with both arms in the air.

I grinned. 'A drive-by.'

Eventually, Gabe skidded towards us at top speed, narrowly avoiding the high-jump equipment, and toppled off the bike.

'Job done?' said Finn.

'Smashed it,' said Gabe, lying out on the grass in a star shape, puffed.

I walked over to him and gently kicked the sole of his shoe. 'So, everyone got their money?'

Gabe grinned. 'Yeah, except for the bodybuilders. But I'll sort them down the gym later.'

Finn shrugged. 'That'll do. Now let's find Mona Lisa and pass on the good news.'

Gabe's arm shot up like a robot's, pointing towards the car park. 'Already located. She's over there, in front of a TV camera.'

Finn's face dropped. 'No way. No bloody way.'

We turned to see a very orange-looking Mona Lisa Murphy, dressed in running gear, posed like an Olympic athlete, fluttering her fake eyelashes at the camera, surrounded by the reality-TV crew.

Finn stormed up to her. 'What the flippin' hell is going on?'

Mona Lisa turned to us, all innocent. 'My promotional interview, as planned.'

Finn choked back the anger, raising his hand in Mona Lisa's face. 'Whoa. Whoa. Whoa. You said that there'd be no interview if we paid everyone back their money. Well, newsflash, it's been quite the payday.'

I grabbed Finn's arm to calm him. 'Wait, what do you mean, promotional interview?'

Mona Lisa raised her perfectly sculpted brows. 'For my sports tanning lotion. The guys wanted to interview a young, successful entrepreneur in the sports industry, seeing as it is sports day and all. Now, beat it.'

Suddenly, I noticed all the bottles of tanning lotion stacked up on the nearby table and the unmistakeable stench of coffee.

I picked up a bottle. 'Your tanning lotion isn't for sport, though?'

'Wanna bet?' said Mona Lisa, pointing to the girls' relay that was about to start. Every participant had orange-streaked legs.

The cameraman pushed us out of the way. 'Stand back, lads. We're filming now.'

We both stood in silence for a minute, observing Mona Lisa as she squirted generous amounts of tanning lotion on her arm and scrubbed at it meticulously, all the while chatting animatedly to the camera.

I bit my lip. Mona Lisa never had any intention of burning us in a tell-all interview. She'd totally outsmarted Finn.

I opened my mouth to speak.

'Don't say it,' Finn said, shoulders hunched. 'I know. I got played.'

This entertaining thought was interrupted by a familiar voice. 'Heads, lads.'

TT Doherty.

He'd fleeced two hurdles from the athletics track and was dangling one on each arm. He spun them like Frisbees, then launched both in our direction. 'I was startin' to think you idiots were avoiding me.'

'What's your problem, TT?' said Finn, sidestepping a hurdle as it came crashing to the ground.

TT flared his nostrils. 'You're my problem, Mr Mohawk. I've come for my cash.'

Finn stepped forward. 'Your money is down the cop shop, TT. If you can get your hands on it, mate, it's all yours.'

TT paused, obviously baffled about Finn's overly mellow attitude to the whole situation. He wasn't the only one. I was left pondering Finn's game plan myself.

'Oh, wait, Luke, what's that sticking out of your pocket?' said Finn theatrically, whipping out the lunchbox and throwing it up in the air, speaking to his imaginary audience. 'Why, folks, I do believe it's a lunchbox, containing – OH, MY – it's a beetle ... Yes, stand back, folks: it's a rare stag beetle.'

TT's eyes bulged. 'My beetle!'

TT made a break for the lunchbox, but Finn was too quick. He lobbed it high over TT's head. I ran backwards and grabbed it, heart thumping.

TT dived towards me, attempting to rugby-tackle my shins, but I drove the lunchbox high into the air and straight back into Finn's open hands.

Over.

Back.

All that throw-in practice at training was finally coming in handy.

Over.

Back.

Within seconds, we found ourselves in a bizarre game of piggy-in-the-middle, with a flaming TT Doherty bouncing around between us, his precious stag beetle being violently tossed over his head from one side of the pitch to the other.

Following Finn's lead, I kept throwing, and tried to ignore the growing urge to puke, as TT's face got redder and redder. Between shots, I wondered how long this could realistically go on for before TT completely lost the plot and slammed one or both of us to the ground.

Finn's arm shot up and he caught the lunchbox with one hand. 'Clear our debts, and you can have the beetle. That's the deal.'

TT froze.

Finn flicked TT a dummy pass, leaving him disorientated. He lifted the lid of the lunchbox and peeked inside. 'Aw, the poor little fella's all battered and bruised.'

TT winced.

Finn slammed the lunchbox shut. 'Fancy another round, Luke?'

'All right. Deal,' said TT quickly. 'Deal, moron.'

'All the debt?'

TT blinked, torn. 'All righ' then.'

Finn fired the lunchbox at TT's feet.

I grabbed his arm. 'C'mon, Finn. Let's do one. Before he erupts.'

TT cocooned the beetle gently in his palms, nuzzling it with his nose and rubbing its back affectionately.

'Nah, look, he's too busy showering the beetle with love,' said Finn.

TT placed the beetle on top of his head, where it burrowed into the mounds of hair, nestling under the greasy blanket. Then he fixed his cap back on his head, scanned the field and made a beeline for us.

'TT, I thought we had a deal,' Finn shouted between nervous backward hops.

'This is payback for my beetle,' said TT, curling his fist, looking like a man possessed.

We legged it across the pitch and along the verge of the athletics track, shadowing the athletes that were competing in the current race. Before I knew it, I had followed Finn onto the track, where we merged with the leading group for some cover.

Glancing behind, I could see TT making ground. He was still pitchside, but quickly gaining on us.

I caught up with Finn, panting. 'What is it?'

'Senior 800 metres.'

The bell rang, indicating the final lap. The leading pack picked up speed. My legs wobbled like jelly, trying to maintain the pace.

Beside me, Finn wheezed, clearly struggling. 'We just need to get to the bend, then blag the race and jump the ditch.'

But I could hear TT's yells getting louder, until it felt like he was in my ear. I held my breath as I waited for the inevitable karate chop to the floor.

But then, a miracle happened.

James Bland, the main contender, came towards the bend, jostling to overtake our group. TT, on the inside lane, was blocking his path.

Bland was livid. 'Move it, slacker. These are the national trials.'

Not content with being a rugby heavyweight, Bland had set his sights on becoming don of the track. But TT wasn't budging. Not for a square peg like Bland.

Bland elbowed TT hard, forcing him off the track. 'Bloody amateurs.'

TT clipped the kerb, stumbled and smashed straight into a barrier, much to the amusement of the lively spectators. As he tried to regain his balance, his cap flew off.

Next minute, TT let out a roar that almost stopped me in my tracks. 'Nooooo!'

I glanced over my shoulder, following TT's horrified trance to a black dot hurtling through the air. As it got closer, I recognised the beetle horns.

The black dot fell directly into Bland's path.

And straight under his foot.

Crunch.

TT watched hopelessly as the beetle, mushed to the side of Bland's gleaming white shoe, was pulverised further into the ground with each stride.

To make matters worse, the runners tailing Bland scuffed the shredded beetle bits off the track.

TT skidded to a halt and plucked a beetle horn from the debris.

There was the briefest moment where our fate hung in the balance. I watched TT's head flicker over and back, almost in slow motion, between the mangled beetle horn, us and James Bland. His eyes glazed over like his brain hurt.

There was a raucous cheer from the crowd as Bland's lead widened. Bland waved smugly to his adoring fans, like he'd already got the gold medal around his neck.

That was the bolt of lightning TT needed.

'Screw you, Burke,' said TT, and split like a high-speed train.

TT sailed right past, not giving us a second glance, all thoughts of his traumatised recently deceased beetle forgotten. He gathered speed, arms and legs pounding, yet hardly breaking a sweat. This was a man on a mission.

Like a powerhouse, he glided around the second corner, then effortlessly drifted around the third, until he was catching Bland down the fifty-metre straight.

I watched the performance, mesmerised. 'He's a flippin' rocket. Who knew?'

Finn slowed, his eyes glued to the finishing line as TT cruised past Bland, urged on by a thunderous crowd. 'Bloody hell, he's only gone and won it.'

$ $ $

We were lying out in the sun, enjoying the last few hours of sports day without the dark cloud of TT Doherty hanging over us.

Finn rubbed his hands. 'TT's forgotten all about us. Too busy frolicking with his fans now that he's the new Usain Bolt.'

A shadow blocked the heat. 'Ahem. So this is where you're hiding, Fitzpatrick.'

I opened my eyes to see Kimberley Farrell, swinging a loudspeaker in her hand. 'Aren't you forgetting something? The big apology.'

Finn snorted. 'Seriously, Kim. You're not still goin' on about that?'

I nudged him. 'In fairness, Finn, she didn't squeal on us.'

Kimberley nodded. 'And I was interrogated by Powder and Miss Shine at least three times about that damn clock.'

She shoved the loudspeaker into Finn's chest, along with a sheet of paper. 'Read this out. It's payback time.'

Unfortunately, at that moment, large numbers had gathered beside our spot for the popular hundred-metre-sprints medal presentations.

Bad timing. Within seconds, all eyes were on Finn, who stood up with the loudspeaker, coughing and spluttering:

'I, Finn Fitzpatrick, apologise profusely to Kimberly Farrell. Kimberley is a kind, funny, amazing person and she didn't deserve the horrific treatment that I dished out to her because I am a complete and utter prat.'

Finn was interrupted by the rowdy crowd.

'G'wan Finn.'

'We all know you're a prat, Fitzy boy.'

'Fitzy, ya muppet, what are ya doin'?'

'Lads, get over here, Fitzy is makin' a plank of himself.'

Kimberley stepped forward. 'Finish it, flake boy.'

Looking more uncomfortable by the second, Finn continued: 'In fact, Kimberley was always far too good for me. I was punching way above my weight when I was lucky enough to go out with her. The reality is that I'm an ug–, ug–'

'Say it,' said Kimberley, enjoying the moment.

'An ugly duckling. And Kimberley Farrell is a – a beautiful swan.'

This was met with a rip-roaring cheer, with the odd wolf-whistle thrown in. Kimberley stepped forward and curtseyed, mouthing 'Loser' at Finn.

37

VIRTUAL REALITY

Finn dribbled the ball. 'Paddy says that Shay Doherty showed up at his door and told him he could keep his damn pigs.'

Koby frowned. 'How'd that happen?'

Finn winked at me. 'Somebody contacted animal welfare. Told them that the pigs were being mistreated.'

'Piggy abuse,' said Gabe.

We all laughed. I'm not sure if Gabe meant to be funny.

I caught the ball on my foot. 'So animal welfare paid Doherty Senior a little visit. Him being the rightful owner of the pigs and all.'

'The irony is that those pigs were treated like royalty. Five star all the way,' said Finn.

'Paddy's given up on the pig videos, though. Too much hassle,' I said, lobbing the ball to Gabe. 'Gone back to his faithful money-making machine: Cedric the Great.'

'Still, at least he got that lug Shay Doherty off his back …' said Koby.

Finn licked his lips. 'Now that the pigs are more useful in a fry-up, Shay has buggered off. Maybe Paddy will throw some sausages our way.'

I smiled to myself. That visit to Lochy's sister at animal welfare had worked a treat. She'd played her part and really put the spooks up Shay Doherty.

Pablo tutted. 'Gabe, what kinda shot was that? Crazy.'

We watched as the ball soared high in the air and over the fence of the basketball court.

'Go fetch, Gabe,' Finn growled. 'And take that flippin' thing off your face. What is it anyway?'

'A 3D visor,' I replied.

'So what? He's gaming on that now?'

I nodded. 'Virtual-reality stuff.'

Finn snorted. 'I think I preferred the helmet. Gabe's terrifying enough without adding virtual reality to the mix.'

I grinned over to where Gabe was running in a zigzag line through the court. 'Probably dodging some gigantic, virtual Angry Birds.'

We sat down, even though the tarmac was melting.

'Paddy will make a comeback,' I said after a minute. 'He's got a lot more balls in the air.'

'Unlike us,' Finn said with a moan.

'Nope,' I agreed happily.

'Paupers. Not a penny to our names,' Finn continued. 'All our hard-earned money vaporised, just like that.'

'At least we escaped relatively unharmed,' I said.

Finn nodded. 'Not like the Filipe brothers.'

'Perishing in some jail cell.'

Koby crossed his legs, eyes sparkling. 'And, you heard what happened to TT Doherty?'

I stretched out. 'Yeah, he's suspended indefinitely. Found with a betting book on school property. And for slide-tackling James Bland at the finish line.'

'Deliberately, of course. Payback for the demise of his beetle,' said Finn.

'Bland's got a broken ankle.'

'Ha. And Bland was odds-on favourite to bring home gold in the nationals next month,' said Finn. 'Not that I care. Bland caused us enough grief.'

I blubbered my lips. 'Powder's high hopes for the athletics team lie in tatters now.'

Finn joined in. 'And his trophy cabinet is still glaringly empty.'

I tried to picture Powder's reaction when he saw his athletics star hobbling towards him. A caged animal would be calmer. 'TT never stood a chance. He got off lightly with a suspension.'

Finn's face tightened. 'TT deserves everything he gets.'

'You traded the stag beetle for your freedom, then?' Koby said. 'With TT?'

'Bum deal,' Finn murmured.

I frowned. 'What d'you mean?'

'I did some online research. The beetle was worth a mint. A good few thou anyway.'

'No wonder you were so cocky with TT.' My jaw dropped. 'Wait, I can't believe you knew this but still gave the beetle away. You've changed, Finn.'

'He's turned his back on the dark side,' Koby said.

Finn kicked Koby on the shin. 'Shut up, idiot.'

'We're still left with one big problem. Powder,' I said. 'He's desperate to sting us for the clock business.'

Finn shook his head. 'Nah, Powder's too distracted now, with his new micro-celebrity status.'

I snorted. 'Hard to believe people actually think Powder's entertaining TV viewing.'

'They should try being on the receiving end,' said Finn.

'He's pulling in the viewers,' said Koby. 'They love him and his wacky suits.'

'Man, he'll be so smug.'

Pablo chuckled. 'Roaming his little fiefdom …'

'Layin' down his laws,' Finn spat.

'It doesn't stop him puttin' the heat on us,' I said, still anxious.

Pablo swiped my arm. 'Hey, at least Kimberley Farrell didn't spill on us. That's a surprise, yes?'

I turned to Finn. 'Maybe she has finally forgiven you.'

Finn grunted. 'She got her apology. Rubbed my face in it too.'

Pablo hopped up quickly, changing the subject. 'What about the disco on Friday? Everyone in, yes?'

Finn threw me a look. 'I'm sure Lukey'll be there, throwin' shapes. What's this I hear about you and my cousin getting together, eh?'

I felt my cheeks redden. 'Do one, Finn.'

Gabe resurfaced, minus the soccer ball, hopping frantically from one foot to the other.

'Gabe, what you at?'

'Playing virtual soccer. See, I'm kicking it now.' He swung his body around, kicking the air. 'Left shot over to my bestie, Ronaldo.'

Pablo looked confused. 'Where's the actual football?'

I pointed. 'Still in that field over there.'

Finn got up slowly. 'Lads, I've been thinking about these beetles – y'know, tropical insects and stuff. I wonder is there money in it? TT planned to sell that one online.'

'Finn, let's just stick to playin' soccer. Here, Gabe,' I said, hopping up to receive the virtual ball on my right foot.

'Listen, I could ask around. See if anyone bites.'

Nobody said a word.

'Kob?'

'Not a hope, Finn. I'm out.'

'Pablo, mate? We could make a killing.'

'No, no, not for me.'

'Lukey?'

'No way.'

'Just think about it, Lukey.'

'OK.' I cocked my head and put my finger on my chin. 'No.'

'All right, all right. Message received. Tough crowd.'